A Ticket to Zion

A Ticket to Zion

A Pilgrim's Progress by Train

Chris Brown

RESOURCE *Publications* · Eugene, Oregon

A TICKET TO ZION
A Pilgrim's Progress by Train

Resource Publications
An Imprint of Wipf and Stock Publishers
199 W. 8th Ave., Suite 3
Eugene, OR 97401

www.wipfandstock.com

PAPERBACK ISBN: 978-1-7252-7098-5
HARDCOVER ISBN: 978-1-7252-7099-2
EBOOK ISBN: 978-1-7252-7100-5

03/08/21

Unless otherwise noted, all Scripture quotations are taken from the New American Standard Bible® (NASB), copyright © 1960, 1962, 1963, 1968, 1971, 1972, 1973,1975, 1977, 1995 by The Lockman Foundation, used by permission, www.Lockman.org.

Scriptures marked NKJV are taken from the New King James Version®. Copyright © 1982 by Thomas Nelson. Used by permission. All rights reserved.

Text in chapters 10 and 33 from *The Seven Redemptive Names of God* © 2017 Dr Peter Gammons, pgmi.org used by permission.

Contents

Acknowledgements

I WOULD LIKE TO thank all my friends and colleagues in the Department for Transport and the rail industry for all that I have learnt about rail systems.

I would like to thank my friends and colleagues who kindly read early manuscripts and provided valuable feedback, particularly Phil Barnett, Mildred Howes, Mary Mills, Andrew Smith, Beryl Murray, Sue Hart, Margaret Lubbock, Michael Kyritsis, and Matt Wimer. I would like to thank Peter Fosdike for assistance with the book's web-site tickettozion.com.

And I would also like to thank Her Majesty the Queen for inviting me to her garden party in honor of my service to the rail industry in the UK and for the opportunity to talk about this book with her as it was being written.

Introduction

JOHN BUNYAN WROTE ABOUT a pilgrim's progress through life to a celestial city. His pilgrim had to walk, but our pilgrim, Ian, has a train to catch. *A Ticket to Zion* is a journey through life by train. Each twist and turn in life is represented as an aspect of a journey by train; the excitement of hearing the first steam train, the joy of being given a free ticket, the horror of seeing so many catch the wrong train, before finally reaching the valley of the shadow of death.

Travel with Ian on this journey and try to understand the station announcements, see how to collect your free ticket, see why life's journey is so hard, and find out its final destination. Ian hopes that his journey's end will be Zion, but will he endure to the end? How many of those he meets on the way will complete the journey, who will end up in the depot, and who will find out they have caught the wrong train?

The author, Chris Brown, was the Rail Research and Innovation Manager at the UK Government's Department for Transport.

This is a mysterious journey. If at any time you would like any hints to unlock the mystery please go to the website: *tickettozion.com*.

And may you have a truly unforgettable journey as you seek to follow Ian on his perilous adventures.

Chapter 1

Ian Takes Tea with Dafydd

IT WAS A DULL, dark winter's morning and Ian wasn't feeling any better. He was run down, like the small Welsh village where he lived. A century earlier it had been alive; alive with the sounds of mining black gold from the hills; alive with the echoes of hymns from the little white chapels dotted up and down the valley; alive with the faces of men blackened by day with the dust of their toil, but cleansed by night with the tears of the Welsh revival running down their faces. But that was a faint memory now.

Ian had just been diagnosed with multiple sclerosis, and he thought he was deteriorating. His mood was deteriorating too. He did not usually get much news from outside the village, and not a lot happened in his village either, but today was different. His cousin Dafydd was coming to see him. Dafydd had lost his sight several years ago in an industrial accident and Ian was looking forward to sharing hard luck stories with him and wallowing in a bit of mutual self-pity.

Dafydd was normally accompanied by his wife Enid everywhere he went, so Ian was a bit surprised to see him arrive alone. On opening the door they exchanged the familiar "How are you—fine—how are you?" greeting, when Ian was suddenly taken aback: Dafydd was examining a rather fine print of John Newton's house on the white-washed wall of the old cottage living room, next to one of Ian's framed Elvis albums.

"Dafydd, you can see!"

"Yes," said Dafydd "isn't it marvelous. Let me tell you what happened."

They sat down on the sofa without even thinking about the nice cup of tea Ian normally offered Dafydd when he paid a visit.

A Ticket to Zion

"It was last Saturday" commenced Dafydd "and I had been invited over to a centenary anniversary event in our village by Andrew Jones, you know, my neighbor. There was a lot of singing—I do love a good male voice choir don't you?—Well, after the singing was over this man from Wapping in England spoke about the Welsh revival; it was the centenary of the revival in our village, you see. He spoke of how tough young miners had been moved to tears as they realized how bad they had been. He spoke of how through faith in God's Son, forgiveness and healing were available to all. Well, I can tell you, I was moved. I felt a spark inside me, right deep down and I responded to the call. How my heart was lifted when I joined in the hymn:

> *Amazing grace! How sweet the sound*
> *That saved a wretch like me!*
> *I once was lost, but now am found;*
> *Was blind, but now I see.*

> *'Twas grace that taught my heart to fear,*
> *And grace my fears relieved;*
> *How precious did that grace appear*
> *The hour I first believed.*

> *Through many dangers, toils and snares,*
> *I have already come;*
> *'Tis grace hath brought me safe thus far,*
> *And grace will lead me home.*

> *The Lord has promised good to me,*
> *His Word my hope secures;*
> *He will my Shield and Portion be,*
> *As long as life endures.*

> *The earth shall soon dissolve like snow,*
> *The sun forbear to shine;*
> *But God, who called me here below,*
> *Will be forever mine.*

> *Yea, when this flesh and heart shall fail,*
> *And mortal life shall cease,*
> *I shall possess, within the veil,*
> *A life of joy and peace.*

Ian Takes Tea with Dafydd

When we've been there ten thousand years,
Bright shining as the sun,
We've no less days to sing God's praise
Than when we'd first begun.[1]

The house where John Newton wrote Amazing Grace.[2] He was born in Wapping
in 1725 and moved to this house in Olney in 1764. He also wrote a preface
to Pilgrim's Progress in 1776.

"And by the end of the hymn I really did feel this amazing grace and
not only that, my eyes had been opened, I was able to see!!"

"So I have decided to dedicate the rest of my life to telling people
about my healing, particularly those in countries who have never heard
about this kind of thing before. I am going to start with Bhutan, you know
next to India and Nepal. I am catching a train there next Thursday from
London, right across Europe through Turkey, Iran into India and finally a
bus to Bhutan. So this will be my last visit to you for a while."

Ian could hardly believe what he was hearing. Then they both remembered why Dafydd had come. Ian went to the kitchen, took out his best tea-
pot from the cupboard and made them both a nice cup of tea, accompanied
with Tesco's finest Battenberg cake. He used to love baking his own cakes,
but since Tesco set up a store in the garage on the main road next to the
village pond, he didn't seem to be able to make the effort anymore.

After Dafydd had gone, Ian began to ponder his words, his new "calling," and the amazing change both to his spirit and to his eyesight. Can anything good come out of Wapping?

The next day Ian was on his way to the shop to see if they had any Welsh cakes on special offer, when he heard a sharp whistle and saw black smoke rising in the next valley just like it must have done a hundred years ago. Ian had never seen a steam train before, let alone a Tornado Mark III loco. He was smitten. But before he could say "Smith Wigglesworth," it was gone.

That night he dreamed a dream of riding the steam train through the dark night up a valley in the shadow of death until it stopped at a col where a beautiful view of a chapel in the sky was revealed as a new day dawned.

Chapter 2

The Special Offer

A MONTH OR SO later Lloyd Jones, the postman, dropped a leaflet into Ian's dark green letterbox, which was perched on a slate wall outside his front door. Normally these went straight into the bin, but just in time, Ian noticed a picture of a train on the leaflet and rescued it from between the potato peelings and an old tin of Baxter's leek soup. It was a special offer to take a mystery train journey leaving the following week. Ian assumed there was no way he could afford it, but then he looked at the small print; it said it was a free offer, the ticket was fully paid for already, all he had to do was collect the ticket from Talybont Post Office before next Wednesday. It sounded too good to be true. It must be a wind-up; his mates would laugh at him if he actually turned up to collect it! You couldn't do anything in Talybont without everybody else knowing about it. Still he placed the leaflet on top of his pile of Elvis albums to think about later.

Ian reminded himself that there is no such thing as a free lunch, as he pondered this "free" offer, and took his daily medicine. How he hated his deteriorating body and this vile medicine he had to take every day! Then he recalled how Dafydd had miraculously regained his sight and was now on his way to Bhutan. This lifted his spirit somewhat. Ian had hardly left his village and had never ventured beyond the border of his native country. He also remembered his fleeting encounter with a steam train the previous month, and his heart seemed to leap as he wondered if the mystery train offer could possibly be a steam train and even be destined to take him to Cardiff, London or even Paris.

That evening at the Fox and Hounds, he mentioned the free offer to his mates. Lloyd Jones the postman was there too. He said he had delivered the same leaflet to everyone in the village and yes, he thought it might be true. He had heard that sometimes they put on a steam train for this trip. It was not part of a Talybont postman's job description to deliver leaflets; he did it as he believed that this journey would be a wonderful experience for any of the Talybont residents, most of whom had not had a holiday for years. Lloyd's expression encouraged Ian to be a bit more hopeful that there might be something in it.

"The dog ate mine." Dai exclaimed.

"I was very excited to get the free train journey leaflet," said Heliwr, his next-door neighbor; he too had always wanted to go on a steam train.

Gerwyn from the farm up the hill said that he was certainly going to pick up his free ticket next time he was passing the post office. So Ian was pleased that he would have company on this journey, if he decided to go.

Ian was still dubious, expecting there would be some hidden charges somewhere, but on the other hand what was there to lose; if it turned out not to be free he could always refuse to pay, he reasoned.

So without a care in the world, the next day he walked down the lane to the post office. To get his ticket he had to sign a form. It was not quite the sort of form Ian was expecting. It was written on bright white paper, brighter than he had ever seen before, hand-written in blood red ink. It already had his name on. The form asked if he was sorry for all the wrong things he had ever done, if he believed in the Train and that there was a train ready to have him on board. He was sorry, and he did believe, so without any further ado he signed the form and received his free ticket. He noticed a little golden seal on the top left corner of the ticket with the letters "HS" clearly visible, otherwise it was pure white and all the lettering was blood red just like the form.

Then, on Thursday, he asked the postmaster how many other people had picked up a free ticket. He was astonished to hear that he was the only one. Dai had had his leaflet snatched away by the dog and he didn't think to ask for a replacement. (Lloyd the postman had a whole stack of them in the post office ready to deliver to anyone who wanted one and he would have happily given Dai a second one.)

Heliwr his neighbor with the red front door had swapped his leaflet for a hot soup that Brwydr (Talybont's star fisherman) had offered him one bitterly cold night last week. And Gerwyn was so worried about his sheep that he couldn't spare the time to collect his ticket. He was in for a good payout for his lambs this year and he was a bit fanatical about ensuring they were in tip-top condition. He also had a bit of a weakness for the local brew (and the local young ladies; in fact the not so young ladies too). So collecting his free ticket came a distant third priority for him. Wednesday had come and gone before Gerwyn had found the time to call in at the post office.

Back home, Ian made himself a mug of tea, sat down, and started to think about what to do with his free ticket. Did he want to go on his own? Maybe it was only a one-way ticket? Would he ever see his village again? Where would it take him? Could he get off the train if he didn't like it? Did he need a passport? What should he pack?

Just then, with all these questions circling in his mind, out of the corner of his eye he spotted a rather nice young lady walking up the lane. She attracted his attention as there were very few young ladies in Talybont, and fewer still "nice" young ladies. She was actually walking straight up to his front door!

The doorbell rang. "Would you like to go on a sponsored walk next week-end?" the sporty young lady at the door said.

"It's for a very good cause." Lilith continued.

Ian used to be a keen fell runner in his younger days and he was tempted to accept the young lady's offer despite his MS. It was not every day that Ian was asked out by such pleasant company.

"Where does it go from and where does it go to?" Ian asked Lilith while trying to look keen, but not too keen.

"Talybont Post Office at 10 am this Sunday, to Zion Chapel and back."

Without thinking any further, Ian said, "You can sign me up; I'll be there all right."

The young lady handed over the form for Ian to sign. It looked remarkably like another form he had signed the other day at the post office, red writing on plain white paper, not quite so bright though, and not quite the blood red of the other form. Then she was gone, on to the next client.

Ian was about to put the form on top of his pile of papers, when he noticed his free train ticket. He examined this a bit more closely and saw that it was a ticket to Zion. "Zion! Where is Zion?" Ian asked himself. "Aren't Zionists fanatics?" Ian's suspicions were raised. It didn't sound like a pleasant holiday anymore. Yet he was also strangely drawn to it, rather like a medieval pilgrim being invited to go on a pilgrimage to the Holy Land.

But the dates clashed! He could not go on this sponsored walk with his new young lady friend and take the train to Zion.

Not long after, that same day, Heliwr from next door knocked on his window. Ian asked him in, offered him a cup of tea etc. Then Heliwr said he had two tickets for a concert on Saturday night in Cardiff at Zion Park, would he like to come. There was an Elvis tribute band, coach, fish and chip supper; normally £50 a ticket, but Ian could have his for £40.

Before Ian could say a word in reply, the phone rang. It was Dai from the Fox and Hounds. He was saying how he would have liked to go with Ian to Zion by train, but had missed his free ticket, however, would Ian be interested in going to Zion by bike, just the two of them after he had sold his lambs at the market? Dai could book a bed and breakfast to stay overnight without any difficulty, just £40? How about this weekend?

That was the third offer in as many hours for an alternative ticket to Zion. Ian's head was beginning to spin. Then to cap it all a dark looking gentleman called Idris stood in the doorway wearing a bright green turban and a white robe.

"Free flights to Mecca," he announced.

"Also cheap extension of trip to go to Temple Mount Mosque in Jerusalem if you like. Here take a look at these tickets! Usually £400, but my Uncle is ill and can't go so I am selling this whole deal for £40 only."

Ian was overwhelmed. What was going on? He had never had so many offers in his life. They all seemed to have some sort of connection with Zion and involve some sort of a journey; the sponsored walk with the nice looking young lady to Zion Chapel, Heliwr's coach trip to the concert at Zion Park, the bike ride with Dai, the flight to Mecca and Jerusalem from Idris, and the "free" train ticket to Zion.

Ian could not decide what to do, he just wanted to be left in peace. He would think about it tomorrow.

Tomorrow came and went.

The next day Ian was up early, he couldn't sleep, so he went out for a walk up the lane—it was a glorious late winter's morning, all the snowdrops were out, the sun was shining, and the birds were singing. Then he heard in the distance a half-familiar tune echoing down the valley. It was Lloyd Jones the village postman (also member of the Talybont Male Voice Choir for the last twelve years) on his rounds. He was singing:

Arglwydd, arwain trwy'r anialwch,	*(Guide me, O thou great Redeemer:-*
Fi, bererin gwael ei wedd,	*Pilgrim through this barren land;*
Nad oes ynof nerth na bywyd	*I am weak, but thou art mighty;*
Fel yn gorwedd yn y bedd:	*Hold me with thy powerful hand:*
Hollalluog, Hollalluog,	*Bread of heaven, bread of heaven*
Ydyw'r Un a'm cwyd i'r lan.	*Feed me till I want no more.*
Ydyw'r Un a'm cwyd i'r lan[3]	*Feed me till I want no more.)*

(For the uninitiated reader the English version is provided too!)

When they met, Ian congratulated him on his rendition and then recounted to him what had happened shortly after he had accepted his free ticket to Zion. Lloyd realized he needed to talk with Ian. Lloyd said "I am just finishing my round, let me buy you breakfast in the café." He then explained to Ian that this often happened after he delivered these particular leaflets. Didn't Ian love trains, wasn't he strangely moved when he first heard the sound of the train and saw the smoke issuing from the funnel? Surely there was only one true way to Zion! Yes, Ian now saw that these other offers were but distractions, and yes, he did believe the train was the only way. So he determined there and then to reject the other offers and take the train to Zion.

Chapter 3

What Time Is It?

THAT EVENING, DESPITE THE uncertainties of the journey ahead, Ian started his packing. Ian had no idea how long the journey would last, nor what to take with him so he just packed a small rucksack with enough things for a weekend. In the secret compartment of the rucksack he placed the gold watch his father had given him when he had turned twenty-one. He emptied his little piggy bank where he kept his life savings (he had never trusted banks and anyway there wasn't a bank in Talybont).

Ian didn't really have anybody to say goodbye to, not even a cat. He had never married and his parents were now dead. His closest relative was Dafydd who was now in Bhutan. So he said goodbye to nobody.

Despite all the excitement of the journey awaiting him in the morning, Ian felt at peace and he slept soundly in his comfy little bed in his pretty little cottage in one of the loveliest villages in Wales. But all that was about to change. Would he regret his decision? Would he ever return to Talybont? Would he ever see his friends and neighbors again? Would they miss him? Would he ever reach Zion, and where is Zion anyway? Ian did not know the answers to these questions but he had made up his mind to go and he was at peace with his decision.

The next morning Ian was waiting on the platform for the train to Zion to arrive. It was due to depart at 07.47 for Swansea. When he looked at his watch it was 07.45. Fine, two minutes to go, time to buy a paper. A minute and a half later he returned to the platform pleased to have purchased a copy of the *Talybont Times* to read on the train. But to his horror the doors had just closed. Through the window he saw the guard pointing to his gold watch; it said 07.46.30.000000002. The guard had been awarded this atomic watch in recognition of his long service and it was his most prized possession.

But Ian had missed his train.

Disconsolate, Ian went to "Information" and asked why the train had left early. "Train doors close thirty seconds before departure," the man said. "But it wasn't quite 07.46.30, according to my watch," Ian argued. The guard on the train had an atomic watch that said it was just gone 07.46.30, but Ian had the same model and it said it was not yet 07.46.30. The guard had seemed rather proud to point to his atomic watch but Ian thought him rather pompous. His attitude seemed to be; "I am right, you are wrong, you are late, I have every right to close the doors and leave you behind." Ian's pride and joy was his gold watch which his father had given him, so he was none too pleased about this guard's attitude, and was about to make a complaint when he heard this pronouncement from the man behind the information desk.

"That is because the train has been to Swansea and back already this morning, after the clocks were synchronized."

"What?" Ian exclaimed incredulously.

Ian declared confidently, "There can never be any connection between what time it is and where you have just been. Surely all clocks tell the same time regardless of the journey they have been on? How can a clock that has been on a train to Swansea and back tell a different time to one that has stayed put? I have studied physics at school; I even got an A, my best subject. I have built lots of different clocks and I have never observed any differences at all."

Then Ian noticed the name badge on the lapel of the customer assistant. It read "Albert." "You have not been looking carefully enough!" Albert said. "It is obvious to me that clocks will tell different times if they have traveled at different speeds," explained Albert. "Look here is proof right in your morning paper, page thirteen, near the bottom." Ian turned to page thirteen and read:

"Time slows down! NPL proves there is a dependence between time and space. NPL is a physics lab where they set standards and measure things very accurately. They took two of their very accurate atomic clocks, synchronized them; one was sent to New York the other one stayed in Teddington. When they compared them they found a difference of 230 nanoseconds between them, significantly more than the accuracy of the clocks (20 nanoseconds). So these scientists proved that time travels at a different rate depending on the speed of the clock. Movement through space affects the passage of time; the dimensions of space and time are in fact connected, but this is only seen by those who have eyes to see.

The blind see! Mr Dafydd Jones from Aber, just outside Talybont, has been reported to have been healed of blindness. This was said to have happened at a meeting in the village a month last Saturday to commemorate the centenary of the Welsh Revival. A man from England recounted stories of the Welsh Revival there a hundred years ago and said that the same miracles could happen today. Several ex-miners from the area reported that they had some sort of religious experience and one of them, Mr Dafydd Jones, was reported to have been healed from blindness. No one from the Talybont medical profession was available for comment. Mr Jones has now left the country for a holiday in Bhutan."

Albert went on to say to Ian, "Most people don't notice, don't care, and don't even try to understand this extraordinary observation. A few, such as scientists at Teddington and at CERN, on the Swiss/French boarder, do understand these things, and use their understanding and their powerful equipment to smash tiny particles together to test models of the universe. Without this understanding, which they call special relativity, they could not do their job. In the same way most people don't notice, don't care, and don't even try to understand the connection between the physical and spiritual dimensions. A few—like those who attended the Aber Welsh Revival Commemoration, do understand, including your cousin Dafydd and Lloyd Jones the postman. Isn't it odd how people can believe that the journey of a clock through space can alter time, but can't seem to contemplate the possibility that someone can be healed of blindness at a religious meeting?"

Ian was now all alone on the platform. Those with tickets had made sure they were on time and had already boarded the train to Zion. Most of the residents of Powys had not collected their free ticket. Ian was the only one from his village to have a ticket, but then he had missed the train! How could he have been so careless, why did he go to buy that paper? It was not worth missing the train to Zion for that! So Ian threw the paper onto the tracks in disgust with himself.

Then there was a voice behind him: "Don't worry," said Lloyd, who had just arrived on the platform to collect the post from the next train and had crept up behind Ian, unnoticed. "The train to Zion will come back for you very soon."

Ian thought that was most unlikely. Trains had timetables to follow, he reasoned, it is just hard luck if you are too late. Anyway how would the train know he still wanted to catch the train to Zion? Surely it would not turn round just for him! But turn round it did. A message was sent to the driver that a passenger had been left behind who still wanted to get on board. So into a siding it went and the engine pushed the train all the way back to the station where Ian was waiting. The signalman made sure no other trains were allowed into this section of track while the train reversed just for Ian.

So after about half an hour the train to Zion reappeared and Ian jumped on with such joy that he had been given a second chance. He listened to an announcement that welcomed him personally on board, and to much cheering from all those already on the train, Ian made his way to his reserved seat by the window in the last carriage of the train to Zion.

Back at the information kiosk Albert was scratching his head. The clock on the train to Zion should have been slower not faster, he reasoned. Also he calculated that the time difference should be only about a third of a nanosecond (assuming the journey to Swansea and back took two hours at an average speed of one hundred km per hour using the time dilation formula that he had discovered: $\sqrt{1-(v/c)^2}$ where v is the speed of the train and c the speed of light).

So Albert too realized that the train to Zion was something special as the guard's watch clearly said Ian had missed the train by twenty nanoseconds whereas Albert expected Ian to be a third of a nanosecond early for the train.

Ian was now on the right train. Or was he? Ian was about to encounter another train, full of people who were convinced they were on the right train. Ian also had a premonition that there was going to be a train crash later that day, but he put the thought to the back of his mind for now.

Chapter 4

The Trainspotters Convention

THE FIRST STOP WAS Abergavenny. The train to Zion was not the only train at the station though. On the other platform stood a "Special." Ian looked across to see what it was doing there, when he spotted someone he thought he recognized.

It was Nick, a member of the South Wales section of the British Trainspotters Association, who was on his way to their annual convention. A special train had been arranged to collect everybody. As the members were scattered all over South Wales, it was a slow train that stopped at nearly all the stations, including Abergavenny.

Nick was just taking a call from his mother. She had been unwell and needed a prescription picking up from the chemist. There was a chemist just next to the station at Abergavenny. Nick was on the platform looking at the two waiting trains—the train to Zion and the special for the BTSA convention which was about to depart.

"Nick!" shouted Ian across the station, but Nick was not listening.

Nick had promised his friends he would go to the convention; there was no way he was going to miss the BTSA special. It only happens once a year, I have a duty to attend, I am a past president, I must go, Nick thought. His mother could wait. Nick had ticked off 665 from his list already and he had his eye on the 666th that he expected to get on the way to the convention. He would then receive a gold accolade from the chief trainspotter. He wasn't going to get diverted by his old mother, nor by Ian, who wanted to invite him to get the train to Zion instead.

The Special was a very safe slow train and although it stopped at nearly every station it did not stop at a chemist, where he could pick up his mother's prescription. The only way to get his mother's prescription was to miss the special train. This train was advertised as the slow but sure route to Sion. Neither Nick nor Ian knew that the train to Zion would have stopped at a chemist (and even delivered the medicine to Nick's mother, if asked).

So Nick got on the Special despite his mother's need and off it steamed. It was full, mainly men, mostly looking like they had left aging parents behind and determined to tick off the next train on their list. The train was called "Tradition of Elders" but nobody could explain what this meant.

A concerned off-duty driver, called Asa from the Train to Zion Rail Company, saw the Special puffing off and was sad that so many had taken this train. There were hardly any on the train to Zion. On the loop where the Special was due to return later that day Asa spotted a broken down van by the side of the track. Carefully and deliberately he took off the brake and let it run down the slope onto the rails where the Special would come before too long! He wanted the Special to stumble without causing a fatal derailment. He wanted all those on the Special to ask themselves if this really is the right train. He wanted to show the whole nation that the "Tradition of Elders" train is not reliable or safe and very unlikely to be able to take its passengers to Zion. He wanted them to realize there was more to life than trainspotting, to leave the BTSA, and join the true train to Zion.

After a few minutes along came the Special to the section where Asa had placed the van. Thud, crash, splutter. The van had halted the "Tradition of Elders." The safety protocols had worked; there were no derailments or fatalities. But the Special could not move, it was stuck. Normally in these circumstances, you would expect a bus replacement service to turn up (eventually) to take the passengers to their chosen destination, but members of the BTSA had signed a pledge not to use busses, so they all just waited, not knowing what to do.

They had stopped next to a canal with a lovely view over the countryside. Before they had time to get too bored a boat arrived and offered a lift to the next station to anyone who wanted (where there was a chemist and where the train to Zion was waiting). An off-duty train driver was the captain of this boat. He urged them all to come aboard, but only a few were even prepared to listen to him. However, Ian's friend Nick had a change of heart and decided to get on the boat and off it puffed (it was a beautiful wooden steam craft). All the others stayed behind and missed the boat.

The captain filled in the passenger list with just one name Nick O'Demus. Nick was safely carried back to Abergavenny train station, where he collected the prescription from the chemist for his mother and persuaded the stationmaster to deliver it to his mother before the end of the day. Nick then boarded the train to Zion with a clear conscience and was surprised by joy bubbling up within him when he spotted his old friend Ian.

"Where is the train going to stop next?" Ian asked Nick after Nick had finished recounting his adventure.

"Cardiff, I think," replied Nick.

"I love Cardiff," continued Ian. "I wonder if there will be time to have a look around?"

"You are going to have quite an adventure in Cardiff," said Nick with surprising insight.

Chapter 5

Announcements

AFTER ABERGAVENNY THE NEXT stop was indeed Cardiff. The train to Zion pulled into the platform and Ian got out to have a look round. Ian was starting to have some doubts about the train to Zion. Where was he actually going? Did the train have to cross the sea? How was that possible? Was there only one train to Zion? What was wrong with the other ways to travel to Zion? Why can't you take the bus, go by bike or plane? Would everyone eventually make it to Zion? What would happen to people who don't want to go to Zion? What if Zion turns out to be for Jews only? Ian thought it time to have a look outside, rather than just sitting in his seat waiting. Nick, being a trainspotter, was quite content to stay put and observe all the trains coming and going from the comfort of his seat on the train to Zion.

Nick worked out that the train was to depart in half an hour from platform seven and the next scheduled stop on the journey to Zion was going to be London. But Ian was gone before Nick had the chance to tell him. However Nick felt sure the station announcements would let Ian know, so Nick remained content observe the comings and goings around the station.

Ian then spotted a rather nice looking café and was tempted by the smell of their fresh coffee. The café was on the other side of the station.

"The neext rain tooo eave . . . form six . . . and wheel be the Oh nine Oh Oh semi-fast to Milford Heaven. Doors will be locked threeee minutes . . . for deeparture. Have an ice day."

This was the first station announcement that Ian had heard. Though "heard" would be an exaggeration, as the sounds echoed round the station like in a vast cathedral and there were so many competing noises that he could not really make anything out. The squeal of trains trying to accelerate round the sharp curves as they left the station, the juke box blaring out from the pub, the buskers trying to attract the attention of passengers rushing past, diesel engines spewing out their unnecessary poisonous fumes as the trains were cleaned, and the noise of desperate passengers queuing at information trying to find out if there was a train to take them home; all this was deafening to Ian.

Twenty minutes later Ian was still sipping his coffee and no closer to finding the answers to his questions about Zion. He thought he heard this announcement: "Some idiot decided that he couldn't be bothered to live anymore so the 09.17 departure from Fishguard Harbour will be 45 minutes late."

These announcers don't show much empathy with the suicidal, Ian thought, as he read a notice advertising the services of the Samaritans on the wall of the café.

Ian had a ticket to Zion not Fishguard, so he stopped paying attention to the announcements and he didn't hear the still small voice announcing the departure of the train to Zion in five minutes time from platform seven. He had also forgotten which platform it was on. Then, when he had finished his coffee, he thought he had better listen out for any announcements about his train. He managed to tune out all the other noises and he thought he heard where he should go. He looked at the information board that told him to go to platform thirteen. The trainline app said platform thirteen too. A member of staff looked up in his PIS (passenger information system) and read out to Ian that all passengers seeking to go to Zion should be directed to platform thirteen. (However Ian thought he saw this man gesture in the direction of platform seven as he was reading out the information, or was it platform six, Ian could not tell.) The station clock was indicating just two minutes before the train to Zion was due to depart.

The previous month there had been an all-staff meeting in which the new improved customer PIS was launched, it was called: "One version of the truth." The idea was for all the different information systems to be fed from a single source of "the truth" so that there was no confusion between the station announcements and what was announced on the information board. The need to correlate this version of the truth with reality was a secondary consideration. All denominations within the company had to repeat the line agreed even if it contradicted what was happening on the ground. This way the company expected to improve its score on "Consistent information communication," and thereby retain their franchise for another generation.

Despite this PIS, Ian finally perceived that the still small voice saying platform seven was the right one and off he set at a leisurely pace, unaware of the urgency to get to his platform. In his way at the entrance to platforms five and six was a vast crowd. A giant information board had been installed there, just where people needed to walk to get to platform seven. The board showed how many seats there were on each train, what color the seats were, when the train was built, the type of fuel used to power the train and also the scheduled departure time and platform.

Some in this crowd had collapsed on the floor, as they were so weary studying the endless information trying to find out the way, the truth, and the life they should lead. Others were pressing forward to get a better view, unaware and unconcerned for those they were crushing at the front of the crowd. There was no way for Ian to reach his platform. Then he noticed the departure time and started to panic.

He tried, "Excuse me," he tried shouting: "Get out of my way," he pleaded with staff to make a way for him through the crowd but all was useless.

Then, with the flick of a switch, the information board lost the mass of useless information and just said: "I am the way, the truth and the life; follow me."

At the same time a bright spotlight highlighted a single figure approaching the crowd from platform seven. He was dressed like a shepherd. He was leading a small flock of sheep with great care and compassion. The sheep followed him because they had heard his call to follow him. They recognized his voice and trusted him. He then beckoned everyone to get on the train that was waiting at platform seven before it was too late.

The crowd didn't know what to do. It seemed rather odd that they should share a train with a flock of sheep! Most were not convinced, some were angry that their right to detailed train information had been denied, others just looked down at their "smart" phones hoping the latest train app would tell them what to do. A few found enough courage to look at the face of the shepherd and when they did they understood in the depth of their souls that this person was indeed the only one who could lead them to where they really wanted to go. So they followed despite not knowing where exactly he was going to take them, but convinced that he would not lead them astray.

Then another message flashed up: "Follow me," it announced in black and white. Then the message board displayed a very impressive video in vivid color, high definition, and 3D. It showed a paradise island with azure sea, white sand, a purple cliff, a green marble hotel with a magnificent swimming pool where drinks of every kind were served by scantily clad young ladies and dishy young men. There was no way to get to this island by train, however. Certainly the train to Zion did not go there. The way to this paradise was different. It required passengers to get into a long thin metal tube that traveled at over 400 mph without a rail track. Its wheels disappeared under two wedge shaped pieces of metal that stuck out of each side of the tube when it departed. It traveled in the sky five miles high where the air was thin and cold. If a tiny hole in the tube were to develop all the air would be sucked out and all the passengers would die. You had to have faith to travel in that. Despite this, each summer thousands of passengers spurned the train to take to the air to explore this and similar islands that promised paradise.

What the advertisement did not say was that the island was so hot you would burn, so remote there was no way off again, and so full of drunk British tourists it felt like hell on earth.

Ian, however, was not fooled. He would take the train. He would follow the good shepherd who promised to lead him to his platform, but the departure time had arrived!

Ian was not alone in his quest to take the train from platform seven. One passenger in the crowd between platforms five and six got out his phone and instead of downloading the train app, he actually used it to make a phone call. He called the Controller direct. The Controller replied and provided him with the information he needed, no more no less. Thus contented, though somewhat embarrassed to be swimming against the tide, this man set off towards his platform and was very pleased to see that Ian too was heading in his direction, platform seven, to the train to Zion which was still waiting for them, despite the fact that the departure time had passed.

Then a rail engineer appeared in a white coat and a hard hat, looking intently at his laptop (which was propped on top of the buffer between platforms five and six). It was showing all the information codes of all the trains due that day, all twenty-seven terabytes of data, billions and billions of noughts and ones, but when correctly interpreted perfectly described the day's train service, and even controlled the movement of each train, automatically generated the announcements (which were pre-recorded), as well as ordering the coffee.

The crowd were still waiting for information on the other side of the barrier to platforms five and six. Nobody from the crowd spoke to the engineer. Nobody had eyes to see, or ears to hear, nor minds to comprehend, nor hearts to appreciate what this laptop was displaying. But to the rail engineer it was perfectly clear that the train to Zion would depart from platform seven and be delayed by fifteen minutes. So off he went, unhindered by the crowd on the other side of the barrier, to ready the train for departure.

Ian and his small band of new companions had made it onto platform seven before the train actually departed; they had passed through the narrow gate that had opened for them when they presented their blood red tickets at the barrier.

Halfway along the platform Ian looked back; he saw the vast crowd of his fellow passengers running and pushing each other to catch the train on platform six which had just been announced, and he shed a tear for them.

Still the train to Zion waited. Ian was not yet back to his carriage on the train. As he ran along the train to find Nick, Ian noticed an empty carriage reserved for children. Perhaps that was why the train was delayed. Before long Ian was to find out the reason for the empty carriage, but before that Ian saw a further commotion on the station concourse.

The crowd had still not dispersed. It was still blocking the way to platform seven. The way to the train to Zion was narrow and few found it.

The next announcement was from the shepherd (who had by now boarded the train to Zion with his flock and about a dozen people from the crowd who had followed him). He left them with this announcement:

"Take the train back to Firstlove, where you first boarded a train, collect your free ticket, have it validated, change trains, and then return here. You have missed today's train to Zion but do not despair, return to where you came from and you will be able to catch the right train tomorrow."

This seemed counter intuitive to most in the crowd, but a kind retired rail engineer explained that when there is a broken down train on the slow line it is sometimes necessary to go in completely the wrong direction, so that you can change onto a fast train that can return on the fast line, overtaking the broken down train. So despite seeming to be illogical at first sight, quite a few from the crowd took the advice, obeyed this announcement, and boarded the train to Firstlove hoping to restart their journey on a better train the next day.

The next announcement was: "The Public Baths next to the Baptist Church just outside the station will be re-opening this afternoon. Anyone who realizes they need a bath and comes to the baths, will be granted free entry, a new set of clothes, a free stay at the five star Station Hotel, and a free ticket for the train to Zion, leaving tomorrow."

By now the crowd were quite sweaty and in need of a bath. They were packed together so closely that it was quite obvious to all that everyone else needed a bath, but it was not obvious to anyone that they themselves needed a bath, so nobody moved.

A new voice made the next announcement. It was an officious sounding voice, not at all like the shepherd's voice. The accent was strange, and most people thought the announcer was not actually from the Rail Company at all. Three announcements were robotically made one after the other:

"Foldable cycles over twenty-seven centimeters will not be permitted on some trains from January 1st. This is to improve comfort and safety for all passengers."

"If you see anything suspicious tell me, the guard. I am currently in the seventh coach of this six car train."

"Due to overcrowding on this service, I will be unable to walk down the train today during the journey. If you need to purchase a ticket you will find me in the tenth coach of this twelve-car train. Please do not hesitate to find me if you require any assistance at all. Thank you."

And then, following these three rather robotic and out of place flawed announcements, a high pitched and somewhat flustered voice made the following announcement:

"Please ignore the previous announcements, the information board, and the train app on your phone. Instead, please proceed to the information desk situated between platforms five and six, where my colleague will be delighted to assist you with any information you may require. Thank you for your patience during this period of disruption."

The "thank you" offered was not in fact warranted as, by now, the crowd's patience had come to an end. They had been told lies, told not to listen to the truth, tempted to catch a flight instead of a train, overwhelmed by a flood of useless information, but the true information had been hidden from them. Now they were being told to queue up at the information desk, where one solitary man would delight in assisting them with information about the right thing to do to get to where they wanted to go. Unbelievable.

Despite being British, and not normally speaking to fellow passengers, suddenly there was an uproar. The whole crowd rushed towards the one man who supposedly could help.

"Off with his head!" they shouted together. Then before they could get their hands on him the transport police arrived. They arrested the man in the information kiosk who was trying to announce to them the good news that there was plenty of room on the train to Zion, that it was free of charge, and today's service was about to leave.

The gate to the train to Zion was now locked and the train was about to leave without them.

The next day the information kiosk was closed. Stuck to the bolted door was a little piece of paper on which was written:

RIP John

Below this there was some graffiti of a severed head on a silver platter. If you looked closely you could just see written in red:

"He prepared the way for you. Follow the shepherd onto the train to Zion and his life will not have been in vain."

Chapter 6

The Child

THE TRAIN TO ZION had not in fact yet left the station. Ian continued walking along platform seven towards his friend Nick, when he saw a child, all alone, going through the gate he had just passed through. He had been separated from his mother. This little lad must have been no more than six, he was proudly holding his own ticket (which looked just like Ian's), which he didn't have to pay for. He had a broad grin, he was so happy and proud, not in a superior way but just pleased he had managed to negotiate the fierce looking gates that would not open even when charged at by a forklift truck. This lad knew that to unlock the gates, you needed a piece of card with a magnetic strip on it that went into a slot made especially for it; then it would swing open under its own power.

Next, the boy's mother approached the gate. She put her ticket into the slot, and waited expectantly, but nothing happened, the gate stayed shut. Alarm spread over her face and she struggled to understand what could be wrong. She knew the train was about to go. She called out to a guard for assistance. The guard slowly opened the mechanism that had swallowed her ticket and extracted her crumpled ticket.

"This doesn't look genuine Madam." the guard explained. "You need to have a ticket like that little lad over there."

"That is my son," she retorted.

"Can't I use his ticket?" she asked.

"No sorry, you have to have your own," replied the guard.

"Well what is wrong with my ticket? I paid good money for that," the mother explained.

"Look I even have a receipt."

"Can I see your receipt please?" asked the guard.

He had seen a good number of forged tickets in his time and he may be able to recognize who had tricked this lady.

Paid the sum of £125,000	
To Chief Deceiver, Head of works of the Flesh and Inventor of Munchausen syndrome by proxy	
Works to the value of £125,000 made up as follows:	
1. Sending my son to Sunday School every week for three years:	£20,000
2. Time spent attending church enduring boring sermons for five years to qualify for a place in the church school for my son:	£1,000
3. Books and CDs about Jesus for my son:	£1,000
4. The best baby food, the best baby milk money can buy for my child:	£10,000
5. A house next to the Church of England school which cost £50,000 more than an equivalent house down the road outside the catchment area:	£50,000
6. Sacrificed holidays so that I could give the best for my son:	£7,000
7. Gift towards a new font at the church next to the school:	£13,000
8. Six months private hospital care for young children to find out what was wrong with him	£23,000

"I am afraid you have been deceived Madam, worthy though all this may have been for your son you cannot buy a ticket for yourself with it. Here take this and go to the office next to platform one."

The guard handed her an application form for a free ticket. All she had to do was admit her faults, ask to be forgiven, and trust the Controller's son to issue her with a free ticket. But was there time for all that? Would the train at platform seven be there when she got back? What about her son?

This presented the mother with a dilemma. Her precious child was on the other side of the barrier all alone. Was she to leave him there in the hope that her application for a free ticket would be successful, when her whole married life had been spent saving for this ticket that had turned out to be a forgery? She froze, not knowing what to do for what seemed like half an hour, though it was probably only half a minute.

The train to Zion was still waiting at platform seven, but it would not wait forever.

"Go get your ticket, like mine," her son called out from the other side of the barrier, "I will wait for you Mummy."

So, fearful for leaving him, and still a bit confused, she finally struck up enough courage to leave her son and fill out the form. With haste she tried to make her way to platform one, but there was some construction work going on around platform one repairing a shop. A sign said: "Do not enter this area without your personal protective equipment."

She had to pass this shop to get to platform one. It was a reptile shop, full of snakes of all different colors for sale to the passers-by. Some of the snakes had escaped and were slithering round the shop floor, then one even sped out of the shop across the station concourse and hissed at this mother, then it struck: one bite, with its jaws buried deep in the heel of this unfortunate lady who was only wearing sandals, not safety boots as advised. But just then a strong looking man dressed all in white approached from behind, struck the snake on the head, and killed it. He also sucked the poison out of the lady's wound before it could do any damage.

Then he said to her, "Here, please accept my ticket, it is for the train to Zion, go quickly before you succumb to any more attacks."

Surprised but delighted, the lady accepted the ticket (which seemed to be still covered with his blood) and ran back to the gate. She thrust the ticket into the slot watched by her son waiting on the other side, and with the sound of a thousand angels ringing in her head she saw the gate open, and she ran through it into the arms of her waiting son.

The three of them were still not on the train though. Ian heard a thud as the gate sprung shut on another mother clinging to her daughter. She had a valid ticket but her daughter did not. She thought that her daughter didn't need to have one herself. She thought her ticket was valid for the whole family. She was quite hurt in this accident and the guard sprinted over to help her. He explained where the free tickets were and what to do to get them. She then asked the guard to look after her daughter while she went to get the free ticket for her daughter.

"No," said the guard.

"She has to go herself. She has to ask for the ticket herself, you can't do it for her."

The mother explained that a man had told her that if he sprinkled water over her daughter's head and said a few words, then she would get a ticket to ride in due course.

"I am sorry to tell you," said the guard, "but that no longer holds for children who can think for themselves like your child, and I am not really sure what good it does for young babies either, but lots of parents seem to believe it is something worth doing." The train continued to wait. How much longer could it wait? Ian wondered.

So after this little discussion, mother and daughter went off to platform one to collect the daughter's ticket, past the reptile shop but right into a massive swarm of flies. A man with a white wig and a red coat, who looked like a cross between Father Christmas and a member of the House of Lords, had just released his swarm. He delighted in frightening young girls. The daughter had been given a stick of pink cotton candy (or candyfloss as they called it in Britain) by her mother to keep her calm, but the flies loved the candyfloss so they made a beeline for it. The daughter dropped her candyfloss on the floor, which was a blessing in disguise as it meant all the flies stayed on the ground leaving mother and daughter free to flee to platform one. The daughter said sorry for this, and for all the other wrong things she had done, then she said she would like to receive a ticket like her mother's. The man giving out the free tickets explained that the ride on the train to Zion could at times be hard and not all her friends would be on it, but she still said she wanted one, so another ticket to ride on the train to Zion was issued, this time with her own name on it, written in blood red writing.

"But will the train wait for us?" asked the mother, knowing it was already late and could depart at any moment.

"I am sure it will wait for you now," said the kindly man who had just issued her daughter with a ticket to Zion.

Nick then spotted a third child leading a motley crew of people from all over the world, speaking all sorts of languages, and wearing all manner of different clothes. They were followed by a selection of different animals that you would expect to be fighting each other (a wolf and a little lamb, a leopard and a small goat, a young lion and a calf, plus finally a cow and a bear). The boy was about twelve. He seemed to know what he was doing. The animals were well under control. The lawyers and priests who were in earnest discussion with him seemed to be impressed. His parents were nowhere to be seen, but he seemed unconcerned about that.

This boy was in fact from a long line of train drivers, fourteen generations in all. Rather like his ancestor he seemed wise and understanding, strong and compassionate, full of knowledge about the rail industry, and most respectful of the Controller. He even settled disputes for adults that could not get on and cases of exploitation of the underprivileged. His words were powerful enough to make a difference across the world and his spirit strong enough to defeat the wicked. He seemed to embody righteousness and faithfulness.

The representatives in the nations who were following him held a flag like a standard as a sign for all the nations to come to him. It was a glorious sight.

Before he boarded the train to Zion himself, however, it was his plan to gather as many of his brothers and sisters as possible from all the nations. They had been scattered throughout the world (into Syria, Egypt, Iraq, and the furthest islands). They had been persecuted terribly for centuries, even by some claiming to be from the train to Zion. He was to assemble these children who had been banished to the four corners of the earth and bring them to Zion. Nothing was going to stop him.

And with that, the guard opened the narrow gate that all may go in. This multitude of people from all nations, as well as the animals, then followed the shepherd boy along platform seven into a special carriage reserved just for them.

A whistle blew signaling that the train was at last about to go, so Nick and Ian stopped looking at what was going on around them, helped the mother and daughter on board, and then jumped onto the train themselves just before it departed for London.

It was the first time Ian had been outside Wales so he was naturally apprehensive, but pleased to be on the right train, and pleased that he was not alone.

Chapter 7

Unhelpful Staff

IAN ARRIVED AT LONDON where the train to Zion would refuel. So everybody had to leave the train and wait in the station concourse. Ian had never been to London, so he thought he would take the opportunity to see the city, not realizing how big it is. All he had time to see was a Macdonald's burger restaurant, a few scruffy men sleeping in abandoned shop porches, and a rather muddy park where a few children were kicking a round ball into a goal (Ian thought that odd as he had been brought up kicking an oval ball over the bar to score a goal). Anyway, when it was time to re-board the train to Zion, Ian approached the station proudly clutching his free ticket that he kept close to his heart. He was surprised to see a long queue. He followed the queue of people into a hall that had the words "ticket office" over it.

There were twelve windows equally spaced on a long counter. Some said "first class tickets only," others said "advance tickets only," and one said "tickets for travel today," which was where the queue ended. All the other windows were closed, despite there being several members of staff chatting away to each other behind the counters, with no interest in providing tickets to the passengers who were queuing up on the other side.

Ian observed the transactions.

"That will be £24,666 please." said the only staff member on duty.

"May I pay with American Express?" replied the expectant passenger at the front of the queue.

"No," replied the ticket officer. He prided himself in his short answers to questions; it speeded up the queue and was thus for the greater good of the traveling public.

"How about Visa?"

"No, this is a cash only queue, can't you see the sign?" Well our hapless potential passenger had not seen the sign and as there was only one window open anyway he assumed a full service would be provided at this window.

"But I haven't got that much cash on me right now," replied the potential passenger.

"There is a bank in the street opposite. Next!" said the officer keen to serve the next potential passenger and get the queue moving again. So off went the first potential passenger to draw out his life savings and then re-join the queue to buy a ticket for the train to Zion.

Exasperated, Ian ran after him and told him that tickets for the train to Zion were free; Ian showed the potential passenger his own ticket as evidence. But this potential passenger didn't believe Ian. He preferred to believe the staff of the Rail Company who had told him he had to pay and the price was a year's wages.

Ian returned to the head of the queue to see what would happen to the next potential passenger. The same thing happened. No ticket was provided and the second potential passenger was sent away to withdraw cash. Ian was now wondering if this staff member was keeping some of the cash for himself!

Then Ian went to the other end of the queue. He began talking to a lady called Nye Eve who had just joined the queue. She was from Jamaica, she was so happy to have made it to the station and finally to be in the queue. She was singing and dancing with joy. She knew the train to Zion was the only true way to travel; she was prepared to pay any price to get on the train. When she had arrived in the UK the rail staff had told her that she needed to pay for a train ticket and she had believed them. Nobody had told her you can get a free ticket to Zion if you ask. She wouldn't believe Ian when he told her; she insisted that you have to pay if you want to travel to Zion. She explained to Ian that it was the best train in the world and that it is worth selling everything you have to get a ticket. She insisted that Ian's ticket must be a forgery. She had labored in the hot fields of Jamaica for ten years, until she had earned enough (the man on the TV said you needed to give 10% to him and use the rest to buy a ticket). Sadly, all Ian could do was to leave her to her queuing.

Puzzled, Ian approached the only staff member he could find to ask why they were selling tickets to Zion for such a lot of money. He replied that it was their job. How were they to live if they didn't take a percentage of the money people were willing to pay to travel? They didn't care that the price had put many millions of potential passengers off. Most staff knew that it was possible to get a free ticket, but they would only mention this if asked persistently.

"Why don't you go out into the highways and byways, and force people to come onto the train for free?" Ian said to one staff member.

"We have been told to stay in the station, where it is warm, where all our friends are, and where we can get free cups of tea, and besides there are no highways and byways here."

"We don't want to go giving away free tickets," said another member of staff.

"My father spent his whole life earning enough for a family ticket and I don't see why others should not work hard for theirs too, even if they have to suffer a bit."

A third staff member, Ben Amitsai was his name, replied to Ian: "I know what the Controller is like, he will not impose the fine for traveling without a ticket, he will change his mind, let people off the fine, and forgive them, if they admit their error, but I think that is unfair, so I am not going to give out free tickets anymore like I used to."

Ian thought the management of the company should know about what was going on, so he queued up at "Information" (a second window hidden away at the other end of the station between platforms thirteen and fourteen).

Ian explained to the lady behind the desk how many people were really keen to go to Zion and wanted to have a ticket to ride, but didn't know that it was free. Surely many could miss the train due to the long wait, the high price or the attitude of the staff. The workers handing out free tickets seem so few and yet the demand so great, Ian explained. Behind the information office Ian spied a multitude of staff in their latter years, in a beautiful garden tending the roses, watering the grass, serving tea to each other, not at all bothered about those passing by getting onto the wrong train, thinking they could not afford a ticket or not even knowing that there is a train to Zion.

Ian was getting no response from "Information." He then spotted a leaflet at the back of the office entitled: "How we spend your money," so he picked it up and started reading. The leaflet explained the revenue and expenditure of the company over the last year. This is what it reported:

TOTAL REVENUE £180m including: Fares	£162m	
Non-fare revenue	£18m	
Made up of: Retail outlet profit		£1.5m
Letting premises for non-rail purposes		£3.5m
Sales of memorabilia		£3m
Car parking		£8m
Lost property and lost persons charges		£2m
TOTAL SPEND £207m, including: Pensions		£121m
Senior management staff costs		£31m
Buildings maintenance (Terminal Stations only)		£9m
Other central expenditure		£5m
Local staff costs		£35m
Seeking to provide free tickets to potential passengers		£6m
LOSS during year: £27m		

Ian had to sit down after reading these accounts. He had worked out that only 3% of the annual expenditure was on seeking to provide free tickets to potential passengers, which was six times less than the company earned on interest on the value of its capital assets (£610m) invested in non-rail purposes. Most of the money was spent on the retired staff tending their roses. Senior management costs were nearly as high as local operating staff costs, and £9m was spent on maintaining the buildings (this spend seemed to be only on the very big stations, where senior management had their offices—local station maintenance did not seem to be important).

No wonder hardly anyone knew about the free ticket offer.

Staff on the trains were no better.

On the way to the main station, Ian had met a friendly looking older gentleman who had just got off a local train during the rush hour (which most rail companies define as from the first train in the morning until 9.30am, i.e. about four hours). The gentleman recounted to Ian the following incident:

"This was the announcement made on the rush hour train shortly after I got on: 'It is impossible for me to move through the train today due to overcrowding. I am currently in the fifth car of this twelve coach train, if you need to contact me to get a ticket, or for any other reason, please do not hesitate to come and find me.' Few attempted this impossible journey to buy a ticket or to ask what time the connection to London was due. Many of the passengers actually had lots of questions. How much do I need to pay for a ticket? What do I need to do to get a free ticket? Was the train to Zion really all first class? How long will the journey take? How do you solve world famine? The staff member who knew most of the answers to these questions was stuck in car five (which had a special compartment for announcers only, a comfy seat, air conditioning, and plenty of room to read the paper). Very occasionally, usually at Christmas or Easter, he would make a bit of an effort and managed to speak to a few potential passengers for the train to Zion, but he had never in his whole career given away any of his pack of free tickets he had been commissioned to give away when he first joined the company."

The gentleman recounted to Ian how he had seen just one brave soul fighting her way down the crowded train, she had one of those badges that gave her preferential seating, and she needed the loo. Most people on the train did not in fact have tickets, they were planning to wait until the end of the journey to buy a ticket without realizing that it would be too late then, as there is a pearly gate that prevents entry to all without a ticket, and there is no way to purchase a ticket there after the end of the journey.

Contrary to the unhelpful staff, Ian explained to the London gentleman that there are in fact many opportunities to receive a free ticket. There are piles of them in waiting rooms, in hotel rooms, and they are even available now on the internet or via the TV (e.g. Freesat channel 695) or radio (MW 1305 in London, or Freeview 725). Free ticket offers arrive in every ones' letterboxes, even in Talybont. Ian went on to explain that there is also a small band of dedicated staff and volunteers, who advertise the free tickets and hand them out freely when they can. Some even sing carols about the free tickets in the bleak mid-winter up and down the land. Some have even testified to the difference the free tickets make to their journey before arriving at the pearly gates: love, joy, peace, patience, kindness, goodness, faithfulness, gentleness, and self-control, as well as healing of their sicknesses when they believe the right person. Ian explained how his blind cousin Dafydd had done just that, how he could now see and that he was now part of this volunteer army handing out free tickets.

Many people even have a copy of a best-selling book in their homes telling them all the details of the free offer, but it is rarely opened, often gathering dust until the day of death approaches.

Children sing songs about the ticket to Zion and have great fun painting scenes from this special book, but more often than not when they grow up they forget about this free offer, thinking it childish and naïve.

Tragic.

Ian then led the London gentleman into the station, showed him where he could get his free ticket, and was thanked profusely for his trouble.

Chapter 8

Gareth Meets Methedig

Ian of course still had his precious crimson ticket that he was clinging on to for all he was worth. He, like many others at this busy London station, was looking for a sign showing the way to the gate-line and onto the true platform for the train to life. Ian had been on the right platform earlier, but had got hungry and curious, so he had left the train to Zion while it was refueling, to get a bite to eat and to see a bit of London.

Ian followed a crowd that seemed to know where it was going. At the front of the crowd was a man in a wheelchair cursing and swearing. He was wearing one of those badges "I love trains," but it had turned yellow with age, the edges were frayed, and it was sagging at an angle of about forty degrees from where it should have been for others to read properly. It did not look like he loved trains at that particular moment. The badge also announced his name to any who cared to enquire: "Methedig Lovelost."

It had been quite a long way along this alley. The crowd had reached the end now. On the left there was a staircase leading down to a set of gates and a glimpse of a train, on the right was another staircase, less steep with a sign saying: "Bar and Toilets." There used to be an elevated walkway with a lift at the end but that had been demolished to make way for a new road.

The man in the wheelchair had obviously missed the sign for the step-free route and was too proud to ask the way, so he just sat there in his wheelchair looking sorry for himself. He was annoyed at the lack of signs and the steps everywhere around him that were like prison bars to him.

In fact, there had been a sign, just for him (Ian had seen it earlier), a special sign showing the route for wheelchair users, pointing to a brand new lift that had been installed at great expense for the 1% of people who were unable to use the stairs to get to the trains. But he had missed it. He had been looking for a square sign with black writing on a white background. His sign however, was seven-sided, gold with red writing on it, and positioned low down at just the right height for him as a wheelchair user.

This man had obviously endured much in life, but had persevered. He had studied hard, got a job, and was now on his way to catch a train for the first time in his life, but he had lost his way. He began to feel jealous of all those other passengers going down the steps on the right to the bar and wished he could get down those steps too. So he turned his wheelchair to the right in a fit of anger and contemplated bouncing down the stairs in his chair to get to the bar below. Unnoticed by him, his badge had fallen to the floor as he had turned away from the steps to the left.

"You have lost your badge." Ian said to him.

"What use is that to me here," the man complained.

Ian could not think of a good reply, so he just said, "What do you want me to do for you?"

"Get me down these *!* steps into that *!* bar!" he replied.

Ian was not sure that was such a good idea, but as Ian was a kind soul he lifted the man up out of his chair and carried him down the steps into the bar. Ian bought him a drink, a burger, and then a coffee. He was about to leave to catch his train when the man asked Ian not to go. He had spent most of his evenings in bars, so he felt at home in the station bar, but he did not feel satisfied with his life. He had just about lost his love for trains (his first love). Then there, in that bar, he finally realized his predicament and asked Ian for help.

"Remember where you went wrong." Ian said wisely.

"Change your mind, do the things you did before when you loved trains, come with me to the train to Zion, I will take you there," Ian offered, not quite realizing what he had committed himself to.

"OK," said the man fed up at last with this bar, "I will come with you to the train."

So, off they went together. Ian gave the badge back to his new friend, and as he pinned it back onto his lapel, Ian noticed that on the back was written; "Made in Ephesus."

With Ian's help his new friend Methedig had found the wide gate for disabled people (which was also for young children in buggies), and his friend had told Ian he would save a place for him on the train to Zion. Ian eventually got through the narrow gate and was on the platform again. He was starting to look for the right train when he spotted an old friend from his school rugby days, Gareth was his name. They had played together for the first XV, Gareth was a prop forward and Ian was a fly-half. Gareth was looking a bit the worse for wear, his Wales rugby shirt was torn and smelt of smoke. Despite hating the state of Gareth's attire, Ian took courage and asked him: "How are you?"

"Fine," replied Gareth, but he wasn't.

"How long have you been here?" Ian asked.

Gareth was afraid to answer this innocent question, because the truth was that he had been on the platform for several weeks, just about surviving. He had collected his train ticket, like Ian, had gone through the gate, but then he had not had the courage to get on board the train to Zion. He wandered around the station platforms, trying to work out which train was the right one to get on. He used to live on the waste food discarded by the other passengers. For entertainment he used to read the discarded newspapers. His prize possession was his ticket. He was so proud of it that he had had it framed in a gold plated frame, and covered with glass so it did not get dirty. Every morning he would kneel down in front of this framed ticket and give thanks for it, but he did not dare take the ticket from its frame and actually use it to get on a train.

Three weeks before his reunion with Ian, Gareth had nearly got on a train. He had bumped into Father Patrick, a priest from his hometown in South Wales. Father Patrick had said to Gareth that he ought to get on the train. The train was called "U Ought 2." It was a very long, inviting train, full of people, but none of them looked very happy to be there. However, before Gareth actually set foot on this train he looked down the line to see where it was heading. Gareth could see that it was heading for a dead end. He could see that it would crash into the buffers. So he said to Father Patrick that he was not sure that he ought to remove his ticket from its frame and get on the train, so he bade Father Patrick farewell and was saved from a tragic journey on the "U Ought 2" train.

Gareth felt sad for all the passengers who had taken this train, which was now heading towards the buffers, but he still didn't do anything about it.

It was about three weeks after this that Gareth had his second adventure. Gareth had got so frustrated with his life that he had broken the glass, snatched the ticket from its frame and started to run to catch a train, any train. Just then a group of fourteen old rugby mates arrived. Gareth had been to school with them and they were all walking briskly for a train called "Twickenham," very much looking forward to the game against England. His friends grabbed him, bundled him onto the Twickenham train and before Gareth could say "Disgwliwch am funud," ("wait a minute"), off the train went, all fifteen of the old school rugby team reunited at last.

The atmosphere on the train was electric, everybody was delighted to be on the train, and most had paid a lot of money for the trip. There was much singing (even including "Bread of Heaven," which Gareth loved), much drinking, and joking (mostly at the expense of the English). It felt good to Gareth to be on this train with his friends. But he also felt uneasy inside, was the train to Twickenham really the right train? But these fears were buried beneath the banter and booze of the rugby special heading to the English temple of rugby.

At first the line ran parallel to the line that the train to Zion was on, but after a few miles the line gradually curved away. It continued to curve away, very slowly, and to most this change of direction was imperceptible, but Gareth noticed it. Eventually it had turned 270°, three quarters of a circle, so that the train was now heading back directly to the two parallel lines where it had started. It looked like there was going to be a crash, or at the very least a serious derailment. But just then the driver spotted some smoke, then he saw a fire, a big fire, right on the line ahead, so he slammed on the emergency brakes, and the train came to an abrupt halt, which shook all the passengers out of their stupor.

Before long the fire brigade arrived, they were all dressed in pure white, which Gareth thought rather odd at the time, surely firemen wore red, but then he remembered he was in England not Wales. But before Gareth had a chance to do anything the firemen in white shouted: "Fire, fire, you are on the wrong train, get out immediately!"

"You are having a laugh!" the rugby team replied. This has got to be an English prank, they thought. "There is no way we are getting off this train, we are on the way to Twickenham for the decider of the five nations; nothing is going to stop us now."

Just a handful of passengers realized the danger and agreed to be rescued by the white fire brigade; Gareth was one of them.

Gareth had had a close encounter, his clothes now smelt strongly of smoke and he noticed his shirt was all torn, but he had escaped. The fire brigade brought those they had rescued all the way back to where they had come from, to the station where all the trains started their journeys. This was where he met Ian and Methedig. Gareth had been snatched from the train fire on the Twickenham train, he had avoided the "U Ought 2" train, and he had resisted the call of his rugby mates to stay with them. Now, at last, he was ready to go with Ian onto the train to Zion, still clutching his red ticket, slightly singed, smelling of smoke but still valid for travel.

That was the end of Gareth's adventures for now. He was safely on the train to Zion with three good friends; Ian, Nick O'Demus, and Methedig Lovelost, the man in the wheel chair from Ephesus.

The train to Zion now left London for the countryside. Winter was nearly over. Primroses were starting to appear, and Ian could see bulbs just starting to poke up out of the little window boxes in the stations he passed on his way out of London. The birds were starting to sing; even the sound of the turtledove could be heard above the gentle clickety-clack of the train. Figs would soon be in the shops, and the vineyards would soon be in blossom, giving forth their delightful scent. "Let us arise, depart from London, and head for the country my love, my fair one," Ian thought he heard from his comfy seat as he drifted off to sleep.

What adventures he had already had, but surely there were more adventures to come before Ian would reach his final destination. Ian was on the right train with three good friends sat next to him and heading in the right direction. Though he had left many behind in London, in Cardiff, and in Talybont, a few had come with him and he was looking forward to the rest of the journey and even more to seeing Zion itself. Winter was over and spring was about to begin.

But, before leaving London, Ian needed to learn where the train to Zion had come from. He picked up a booklet called "To Coventry and Back," and read all about the extraordinary history of the train to Zion.

Years ago the train to Zion had been up north, in Coventry. There had been an argument on the train between twelve brothers. Their father had put his favorite, Jake, in charge, but the others resented it and tried to do away with him. Jake escaped to Coventry and made a fortune when he set up a new agricultural equipment business there. The other brothers stayed down south where there was a bad recession. Eventually they all decided to go to the Midlands where they could at least get unemployment benefit. They were surprised to find their brother there, not only running his own business, but virtually the whole local economy. Jake had been appointed chair of the East Midland Chamber of Commerce, and all he did was incredibly successful. So, after saying sorry for the way they had treated

Jake, the family were reunited and settled down in the countryside near Coventry tending sheep.

The train to Zion had gone to collect them, but the way to Zion was not yet clear and the train ended up staying for more than 400 years stuck in Coventry. Prosperity from sheep farming evaporated. They became more like slaves and their children were forced to construct a new motorway round Birmingham. They started to feel very sorry for themselves. They had not had a holiday for three long generations. But then they remembered Zion, they remembered they were not really from Coventry at all. The controller of that land had ordered all the children of Jake to be killed. However, Moshe, the great, great, grandson of Jake, was saved and rose up to free his people from their servitude.

Chapter 9

The Hail Storm

IT HAD BEEN A terrible few months. In fact the last 430 years had been pretty bad, according to the booklet Ian was reading. The train to Zion was timetabled to depart from Coventry for a three day special. This was called a holiday, but most people on the train had forgotten what a holiday was. Moshe, the new driver, had announced that the train would be leaving shortly. But the controller of that county had instructed all signals to be set to red. No trains were leaving Coventry. Then Moshe marched right into the controller's office and demanded that the signal be changed to green, if not there would be a sign from the real train maker. The controller said, "No." So Moshe declared the first sign, he said; "Listen, let the train go! By this sign you shall know who runs the train; this river over there will be turned red like your signals," and out he went.

The next day the River Sherbourne had turned to blood and all the fish were dead.

A week later Moshe returned to the controller and announced: "Let the train go, or the land will be covered with frogs." And the land was covered with frogs; they even ended up in the controller's bedroom. The controller's wife wasn't too keen on frogs in the bedroom and made her feelings known to her husband. So the controller called Moshe back and said, "OK then, I will let your train go, only ask the maker to get rid of all these frogs." Moshe said, "Fine, it will happen tomorrow." So Moshe sent a request to the maker to dispose of the frogs and they were all gone within the day. But the signals remained red.

"Insects!" Moshe said to the controller. "But there will be no insects in the train." The local controller replied: "OK then, I will let the train move, but only within the confines of Coventry; you don't have a certificate of conformity to the Technical Specifications for Interoperability, so you can't cross a county border."

"But we must follow the instructions of the maker who told us to leave Coventry on a three day journey," replied Moshe. "The fourth sign for you, and for the entire world's media, will be boils on your livestock. They will be dead tomorrow but none of our animals will have a single boil on them." Still no permission to depart came. So Moshe returned to the Coventry controller again and explained why all this was happening. Moshe explained it was to show him, and the whole world, that the maker was who he said he was—the maker.

Next Moshe announced a hailstorm.

Every other word from Moshe had come true exactly as he had announced beforehand, so you would have thought that by now the Coventry controller would have got the message and realized he had met his match. "You better stay under cover!" advised Moshe.

The Coventry transport communications team re-tweeted this message from Moshe and within thirty seconds it went viral. Everybody knew a hailstorm had been announced by Moshe and that it would arrive the next day.

There was quite a crowd at the station where the train to Zion was stuck behind the red signal. The announcement had been made repeatedly that a big hailstorm was coming towards the station and the sky was indeed getting blacker and blacker.

There was a large waiting room on the platform with two trains waiting to leave. The trains looked similar but one was heading for Zion and the other one to who knows where. The train to Zion was smaller, but clean and bright, the other train was bigger, dirty, had no windows, and appeared superior to its companion, proudly, almost arrogantly, looking down on the train to Zion.

The passengers in the waiting room had a choice to make. These were the choices available:

1. Get on the train to Zion

2. Get on the other train

3. Wait in the waiting room

4. Return home quickly to shelter in their own homes

5. Deliberately stand out in the open away from shelter to make a point, or

6. Block their ears so as not to hear any more announcements and stay put.

It started to rain. Then the sun came out and everyone saw the most beautiful triple rainbow.

A Sunday School group then arrived on the platform, which by now was getting very congested. People had not yet made up their minds what to do and the storm was approaching. The Sunday School children all heard the station announcement to get on the train to Zion, so on they got. However, a "guard" was on duty from the other train and asked all the children to get off as they tried to sit down on the many empty seats. "These seats are reserved," he said. "This one is for the Archbishop of Alexandria; this one is for the Bishop of Coptos. Dr Penthu was sitting in this one and he has just popped onto the platform to see if he can help." So the children all moved into the next carriage. The "guard" followed them. "You can't sit there," he said, "this carriage has blue seats and you have not got the right tickets." The Sunday School superintendent argued that the carriage had been declassified a long time ago and was free to all now, even children on their own, but the "guard" was having none of it. He had been taught on his train that blue seats meant first class and that first class tickets had to be shown to gain admittance, no exceptions. So off they went to the next carriage. This had no seats at all, but the children did not mind. There were a couple of bikes in one corner and a large case in another, but other than that there was nothing in the carriage, so there was plenty of room. They rather liked it, plenty of room to play they thought. A group of three cyclists then arrived with their bikes. "Sorry you are not welcome here," they said to the children, "you might run around and topple our bikes over, or start singing or dancing and disturb our journey, off you get now." So rather reluctantly they did as they were told.

It was raining quite heavily now and the Sunday School party did not have any coats with them so they started to get wet and cold. They starting banging on the train doors but tragically nobody would let them in. They started running up and down the length of the platform, scattering the people on the platform as they went. A few of them were adopted by a big family and bundled onto the other train. Others were chaperoned into the shelter of the waiting room by their parents who had by now arrived and were looking for them. Others carried on running up and down the platform despite sharp words from their parents and the "guard." Finally an old couple opened the door to the train to Zion, took hold of two little orphan girls by the hand, and found them a place next to where they had been sitting previously. They were saved, safe now back on the train to Zion.

Chapter 10

The Waiting Room

THE WAITING ROOM WAS full now. It was warm, a little smelly, and not really equipped for accommodating such a large crowd. However, round the walls there were many leaflets, neatly folded in specially made containers.

A very well dressed man, Davidson was his name, had just arrived in the waiting room. He noticed the leaflets. He was a retired Speaker of the House of Commons. He examined the leaflets and counted them; there were twenty different leaflets around the room. They all had the same title, "What to do in the event of a hail storm." That was convenient Mr Davidson thought and started to read them one by one.

Starting with the first leaflet Mr Davidson set his mind to seek and explore by wise analysis all that has been done for those in the waiting room.

1. HAIL STORMS: FACTS & FIGURES

The first leaflet that Mr Davidson read was obviously written by a statistician.

The largest recorded hailstone in U.S. history fell on July 23, 2010, in Vivian, South Dakota, measuring eight inches in diameter and weighing 1.94 pounds. The prized stone is now on ice at the National Centre of Atmospheric Research in Boulder, Colorado. There were 5,457 major hailstorms in the USA in 2013. In Australia on 14th April 1999 a storm struck the city's eastern suburbs of Sydney. This storm dropped an estimated 500,000 tonnes of hailstones in its path causing fifty injuries, but no deaths. There have been reports of one child dying from a hailstone strike in 1893 and another in 1928.[4] Approximately five people die over a century from hail in the USA. There are about 300 million people in the USA, so the probability of death from a hailstone, in any one day, is one in two thousand billion.

So you are safe to leave the waiting room, very probably.

Then Mr Davidson noticed a footnote to this leaflet.

Say evolution requires 200 successive mutations to produce an entity that can reproduce itself i.e. life from the remnants of stars. Assume that, at each mutational step, there is equally as much chance for it to be good as bad. Thus, the probability for the success of each mutation is one in two, or one-half. The probability of 200 successive mutations being successful is then $(\frac{1}{2})^{200}$, or about one chance in 10^{60}.

Let us imagine that every one of the earth's 10^{14} square feet of surface harbors a billion (10^9) mutating systems, and that each mutation takes just half a second. This is thus about 10^{39} attempts to mutate over 10 billion years. So the probability of a 200 component organism evolving over the last 10 billion years is $10^{39}/10^{60}=10^{-21}$. All this means that the chance that any kind of 200-component integrated functioning organism could be developed by mutation and natural selection just once, anywhere in the world, is less than one chance in a billion trillion.

So if you believe in evolution you had better stay in the waiting room.

2. THE WAITING ROOM: HOW TO ENJOY YOUR STAY

This leaflet explains where the snack dispenser is and how it works. It advertises the soft drinks machine (sponsored by Coca Cola) and, in small letters so children cannot read it, where the bar is located.

It signs off with a merry ditty, "Eat, drink, and be merry for tomorrow you die."

3. THE TRAIN TO ZION: GOOD NEWS

This leaflet contains good news.

God loved you so much that he gave His Only Begotten Son to be your savior. On the cross, Jesus died bearing your sins, so you could be forgiven and have eternal life

Only Jesus can save you. You cannot save yourself. Our sins caused a separation between us and God. But Jesus died in our place on the cross, and was raised from the dead, taking the punishment that we deserved, so that we could be forgiven

Salvation is God's free gift. It is yours for the asking. Do not put it off any longer. The past is gone forever. The future is uncertain. Now is the day of salvation.

Peace with God is freely available to you right now if you will receive Jesus Christ.

Everyone will one day stand before God, and give account of whether they received or rejected Jesus Christ.

This leaflet also contained a prayer:

Lord Jesus Christ, thank you that you love me, thank you that you died for me and then rose again to give me new life. I believe that you took the punishment for my sin so that I could be forgiven. Forgive me right now. I invite you to come into my life to be my Savior and my Lord. I confess with my mouth that Jesus Christ is Lord, and believe with my heart that God has raised him from the dead. I thank you that you have heard my prayer. I am forgiven, I am saved. You are mine! I am yours . . . for all eternity! In Jesus name, Amen![5]

You are on the train to Zion.

4. THE TRAIN TO ZION: GOOD NEWS

This leaflet contains good news:

> The good news (or gospel) is the singularly most important communication of God to man. In Jesus, who is God the Son, we have the revelation of God's love and sacrifice that saves us from God's righteous judgment upon sinners.
>
> The Bible tells us what the gospel is in 1 Cor 15:1–4,
>
> "Now I make known to you brethren, the gospel which I preached to you, which also you received, in which also you stand, by which also you are saved, if you hold fast the word which I preached to you, unless you believed in vain. For I delivered to you as of first importance what I also received, that Christ died for our sins according to the Scriptures, and that He was buried, and that He was raised on the third day according to the Scriptures."

The Bible says we are all sinners (Rom 3:23). This means we have all offended God. We have all broken His law. Therefore, we are guilty of having sinned. Because of this, we are separated from God (Isaiah 59:2), are dead in our sins (Rom 6:23; Eph 2:1), cannot please God (Rom 3:10–11), and will suffer damnation (2 Thess 1:9). The only way to escape this judgment is by receiving Christ, by trusting in what Jesus did on the cross (John 14:6, Acts 4:12; 1 Pet 2:24).

Since we are sinners, we are incapable of removing the guilt of our sinfulness through our own efforts. Gal 2:21 says, "if righteousness comes through the Law, then Christ died needlessly." The Law is the dos and don'ts of moral behavior. In other words, we can't become righteous by what we do. Why? Because we are dead in our sins (Eph 2:1).

This means that since we cannot remove our own sins, God must do it. Jesus, who is God in flesh (John 1:1, 14; John 8:58, Col 2:9), bore our sins in His body on the cross (1 Pet 2:24). He died in our place. He paid the penalty for breaking the law of God that should have fallen upon us. He satisfied the law of God the Father by dying on the cross.

It is only through Jesus that we can escape the penalty that God will execute upon all who have broken His holy and perfect law. Do you want to be saved from the righteous judgment of God? If so, if you want to become a Christian and follow God, then you must realize that you have sinned against God, and are under His judgment. You must look to Jesus who died on the cross, and trust what He did in order for you to be forgiven of your sentence, and be saved from the judgment of God. This is accomplished by faith alone in what Jesus has done. You cannot add any human works to what Jesus has done.[6]

You are on the train to Zion.

5. ZION

This leaflet was headed with the Star of David:

Zion is a hill in the older part of Jerusalem, and is often called the city of David. Zion literally means fortress. The Sidonians called it Mount Sirion (which sounds a bit like Sion).

The daughters of Zion are promised salvation (through a king that is coming to them, a just king, endowed with salvation). So they don't need to fear, they can be saved from the hailstorm if they trust the king, the maker of the train to Zion. This king will speak (declare, create) peace to the nations, he will be able to calm any storm. His dominion will also reach to the ends of the earth (so, well beyond Jerusalem and the land of Israel). The daughters of Zion will be called "The holy people, the redeemed of the LORD."[7]

There is, however, a stone of stumbling in Zion. It is both a rock of offence (to those who will not believe, but instead trust in their own efforts, but also a way of removing shame to him who does believe in him (the coming king), no longer being stressed, disappointed, or disturbed. This stone is called faith.

The Deliverer will come from Zion and he will remove ungodliness from Jacob. The agreement is that he will take away their sins.

The Redeemer also comes *to* Zion as well as *from* Zion. He will come to those in Jacob who turn from transgression.

So it looks like the maker of the train to Zion came from Zion, and is returning there again, having created peace on earth and removed sin, he will take any on board who have faith in him.

6. SUBMISSION

The way to be saved from the hailstorm according to this leaflet is by submission, or in Arabic "Islam". To signify this submission the following five things must be done:

i. Say frequently "There is no god but Allah, and Muhammad is the prophet of Allah."

ii. Pray five times a day after washing, and in the right direction

iii. Fast during the day for one month of the year

iv. Give 2.5% of your wealth to the Muslim poor, and those who fight Jihad

v. Make a pilgrimage to Mecca, if you can afford to, before you die.

7. SUBMISSION

The way to be saved from the hailstorm according to this leaflet is by submission, or in Arabic "Islam". To signify this submission the following five things must be done:

i. Say frequently "There is no god but Allah, and Muhammad is the prophet of Allah."

ii. Pray five times a day after washing, and in the right direction

iii. Fast during the day for one month of the year

iv. Give 2.5% of your wealth to the Muslim poor, and those who fight Jihad

v. Make a pilgrimage to Mecca, if you can afford to, before you die.

Davidson was a bit puzzled. Why were there two leaflets headed "Submission," which to him looked exactly the same?

8. THE WATCH TOWER

This leaflet at first sight looked to Mr Davidson like leaflets 3 and 4. However, on more careful reading, he noticed that there were a number of additional features.

> "Jehovah Witnesses believe that the kingdom of God is a real government in heaven that will soon replace human governments and accomplish God's purpose for the earth. They believe that Jesus is the King of God's kingdom in heaven and that he began ruling in 1914. A relatively small number of people—144,000—will be resurrected to live with Jehovah in heaven and rule with Jesus in the kingdom. They believe that God will bring billions back from death by means of a resurrection and that 'many now living may yet begin to serve God, and they too will gain salvation.' However, those who 'refuse to learn God's ways after being raised to life' will pass out of existence forever."[8]

9. INSTRUCTIONS FOR THE TV

Turn on the TV using the switch on the wall by the window. Sit back and enjoy the programs. The storm will pass, so don't worry.

10. NIRVANA AFTER THE HAILSTORM

Everybody will experience a hailstorm, but don't worry; everybody will be reincarnated after that. The state that you re-emerge will depend on what you have done. You could return as a Bollywood star or as an ant. Eventually you will return and lead a good life, and then reach Nirvana.

11. A GUIDE TO A CHRISTIAN APPROACH TO LIFE IN THE WAITING ROOM

A good Christian should be nice to others, visit the sick, attend church, give to charity, be christened, confirmed, and finally buried. Be patient as you wait here. There is no need to be "saved". The maker of the train will see all the good you have done, and save you from the hailstorm, if there is one. There are many books you can read to gain enlightenment and guidance. The Bible is one of them, and although it contains some myths and strange stories, it is still helpful to read as you wait here in the waiting room. There are many roads to Rome. The train to Zion is not the only way. Are you sure you want to go to Zion, is not Rome a better destination for many? You do not need to mind the gap to get to Rome. You do not need to admit that you have sinned against God. Surely God is a good God and will have mercy on everybody, especially those who wait patiently here, and are as nice as they can be in the circumstances to the other people waiting here.

12. SEX, DRUGS, AND ROCK AND ROLL

There is a red door to an X-rated room next to this waiting room. This leaflet allows you admission; please bring a friend (or two). We promise you a good time, and you will hardly notice the hailstorm in there. Go on, give it a go!

Once you are in there, you won't want to come out again as the X-room is specially designed to be very difficult to escape from, so expect a long stay. You don't even need to think about getting on a train in there. In fact it is so loud you can't even think at all.

13. THE TOILET

The toilet is situated to the left as you enter the waiting room. Go there now. Flush all of life's shit down the toilet. Vomit up all your life's work. Then you will feel better.

14. CHILDREN IN THE WAITING ROOM

The most important people in the waiting room are the children. They are the future of the world. Don't worry about saving yourself from the storm; make sure they are safe first. Make sure they go to a good school, do their homework, make nice friends, say "Please" and "Thank you," tidy their bedrooms, and pass all their exams (or if they can't, teach them to win at sport). Try not to let them watch too much TV or play X-box all day. If you do all this, then when the waiting room collapses under the impact of the hailstones, they will be safe and cozy.

15. HAIL STORM MYTHS

All the other leaflets in the room are just myths. There is no way to know how to survive the hailstorm. The rest of this leaflet is left blank for you to write your own plan. Good luck!

16. THERE IS PLENTY OF ROOM FOR ALL
IN THE WAITING ROOM

This is a large waiting room. There is plenty of room for all here. God won't let you die in the storm, it won't be that bad. God is good, he will not judge anyone. There is no need to get on a train. Just wait here until the storm passes. Even if this shelter collapses, the worst that can happen is that you get a bit wet. You will dry out. Those signs of frogs, the river turning red, and dead cattle, were just a con, an illusion, don't fall for it. Don't believe those announcements that you need to get on the train to Zion. Ride out the storm here with everybody else.

17. THE CASH MACHINE

Work hard, earn all you can, then you will be able to build for yourself and your family a nice solid shelter. You won't need to share this waiting room with all these people anymore. The cash machine is situated at the other end of the platform. It contains limited cash so make sure you get there first, and don't worry about pushing the others out of the way to get there— your ambition, your drive, your hard work, deserve rewarding. Those lazy people sitting around in the waiting room don't deserve to get to the cash machine first, push them out of the way if they slow you down, and don't tell them where it is!

18. YOGA CLASSES

Yoga classes are held every third Thursday at 8pm in this waiting room. Please vacate the room ten minutes before the start of the class.

19. WHEN WILL THE STORM COME?

The big hailstorm will arrive on the 13th day of the 8th month in the year 666.

20. ENGINEERING WORKS

This shelter is unsafe. It only offers temporary shelter in mild storms. It has been vandalized. Get the train to Zion as indicated in leaflets 3 or 4 as soon as possible. Do not wait in this waiting room any longer.

Mr Davidson picked up leaflet number 12, went in the back room, and was never seen again. The key to the waiting room was given to his son Rehoboam, who threw it away. Abijam, his grandson, picked it up, and it remained in his family for many years, until the Controller's son came and built a new building, after which the waiting room was no longer needed.

Chapter 11

The Promised Land

THE TIME HAD ARRIVED for the train to Zion to leave Coventry. The promised hailstorm happened. Those who had believed the announcement of the great storm took shelter in their homes or in the waiting room, and survived, but those who paid no attention to the announcement suffered great loss.

Then the controller of the county of Coventry called for Moshe, said "Sorry," and agreed to let the train to Zion depart. So Moshe prepared the train to leave Coventry, but the Coventry controller changed his mind yet again. Moshe returned to announce a plague of locusts. All the people of Coventry then called on their controller to let the train go, but still he imposed unacceptable conditions for the train to depart. So darkness fell over Coventry, and then those on the train to Zion were told to do what seemed a strange thing. They were to hold one last meal in Coventry, roast lamb with flat bread, and they were to place some of the lambs' blood on the outside of the train-doors.

The next morning all the first-born sons in Coventry were found dead, apart from those who were on the train to Zion. All the people of Coventry wanted rid of the train to Zion now. They were even prepared to give all their gold and silver jewelry, as well as their best clothes, to those on the train to Zion, as a parting gift.

So, finally the train left. It was heading for the Promised Land, but where is the Promised Land? The train seemed to be taking a strange route. It was being pursued by a diesel train from Coventry sent to recapture their gold and silver, but Moshe drove the train to Zion through what seemed to be a sea of reeds, and miraculously it made it to the other side. The pursuing train did not make it across.

On leaving the East Midlands they did not arrive in the Promised Land straight away. The passengers started to grumble because there was nothing to drink. So Moshe stopped, hit a particular rock with a stick, and out flowed a stream of fresh water for them to drink. Then they complained about the bread, even though it was made for them fresh every day, and tasted like waffles and honey. Then they complained about lack of meat, so Moshe asked the Controller to send meat, and before long they were knee deep in quails!

One day, when the train had stopped at the bottom of a high mountain, Moshe got out, and was gone for forty days. The passengers on the train thought he must be dead, and elected a new driver, who used the gold they had been given when they left Coventry to make a model of a cow as a bit of a joke, for they could hardly remember what beef tasted like. But to their embarrassment Moshe turned up, and he was not in a good mood. He smashed their golden cow, as well as a new set of instructions he had been given by the Controller while he was on the mountain.

When they arrived at what was supposed to be the Promised Land, they were not too impressed. There were giants there who were so powerful the passengers considered themselves like grasshoppers in comparison. Only two people (Josh and Caleb) out of the original two million saw the positive, and urged the train to go on. So Moshe turned the train round, and headed back towards Coventry. The journey was so long that the entire generation of the moaners died out. Of the original two million only Josh and Caleb were left alive. Even Moshe didn't make it, because he had disobeyed the Controller's command. For when the passengers were dying of thirst, he struck a rock with his stick, thinking that water would flow out as it had done previously. But it didn't, because this time he had been told to just speak to the rock, in the presence of all the passengers. This was the first time Moshe had diverted from what the Controller had said, and it cost him his job. (Despite his disobedience however, water was graciously provided to all the people when he hit the rock a second time.)

So just two of the original two million entered in, together with a new generation of passengers. Josh was the new driver, and Caleb the new guard.

After another amazing ride through the River Thames, that just happened to be dried up at the time, the train arrived in London, which is where Ian, Methedig and Gareth boarded the train. Ian continued to read the booklet about when the train to Zion went to Coventry and back. The streets were not in fact paved with gold, it was already full of people, but none of them were there to welcome the arrival of the train to Zion back to the capital.

It took another fourteen generations of drivers from the time of Ab (Jake's grandfather) to David before the rail system was fully established in the capital. It was just after David's time that Temple Station was built, a great and wonderful station, probably the most beautiful in the world. After David died, the Rail Company divided into two parts, Southern Rail and Northern Rail. Northern Rail was not connected to London, and soon lost popularity. Both companies struggled on for nine generations with a mixture of good and bad drivers, before a particularly bad driver took charge of Northern Rail. He was heavily influenced by his wife Jez, who hated trains; she always traveled by car, and tried to persuade her husband to give up traveling by train.

But there was more to the crew of the train to Zion than a succession of bad drivers . . .

Chapter 12

The Crew

IT IS TIME TO get to know the crew of the train to Zion. Ian worked out, from reading the booklet, that there were probably three types of crew; drivers, cleaners, and announcers. Clearly the drivers drove the train, but as the train had to follow the tracks, and the route was set by the Controller, to Ian, the driver seemed to have rather limited power, though he (or, very occasionally, she) could determine the speed of progress towards the goal, and where to stop to let passengers on and off, as it was the driver who had control of the brakes and the doors (or was that the announcer's job?). The cleaner's role was obviously to keep the train clean, which would be an easy job if it wasn't for all the passengers who kept leaving rubbish all over the place, putting their dirty feet on the seats, and sometimes being sick, and not always in the proper place.

And the announcers made the announcements. Though Ian was beginning to doubt even this, as he had noticed that often the announcements were exactly the same; the same words in the same tone of voice; "Mind the gap, stand clear of the closing doors," and sometimes the message was completely inappropriate. Once there was an announcement when the train was speeding down a hill; "This train is out of service and returning to the depot, please leave as soon as possible by the nearest door." Ian suspected that some announcements were in fact pre-recorded and were just being regurgitated on the press of a button, and sometimes the wrong button was pressed. These announcers also called themselves guards, but Ian had never seen anyone doing any guarding of the passengers.

So Ian was curious to meet the drivers, the cleaners, and the announcers. So, he put down his booklet and went in search of them.

The first crew member Ian met was an announcer. He wasn't wearing a uniform. In fact he was dressed rather oddly in a camels' hair jacket, and a leather belt. He said his food was honey and locusts! His job was to make announcements about things before they happened, and to pass on messages from the Controller. He said he was the last of the announcers. His name was John Grace Make-Ready. Ian seemed to remember a John who had died giving out information about free tickets to Zion at a station in London. Could this be the same John? It didn't seem to make sense to Ian, as this man was so full of life.

Ian asked John what it was like to be an announcer. John took this as an opportunity to recount some famous incidents from former announcers' lives.

This is what John recalled to Ian and his three friends (Gareth, Nick, and Methedig), as the train rattled its way along its tracks towards Zion: "At first, the announcers gave clear straightforward announcements like; 'This train is for Zion, please make it known throughout the world that everyone is welcome on this train,' but the passengers didn't pay much attention, and after a short while, they blocked their ears with headphones and loud music, or just 'zoned out,' by burying themselves in their newspapers.

"The Controller really wanted lots more people on his train, so he sent other crew to run the train service; charming ones, loud ones, quiet ones, funny ones, sad ones, northerners, southerners, westerners, easterners. But nobody seemed to be listening. Proof of this was a massive warehouse full to the brim with umbrellas, coats, hats, mobile phones, and even the odd bicycle. Every announcer had made the announcement to ask passengers to check that they take all their personal possessions with them before leaving the train. The full warehouse confirmed that many had not listened, or not understood the message of the announcers."

John continued his discourse to Ian about the history of the rail industry. "Other announcers had announced changes to the service; few listened. Later there were warnings of major disruption, even deportation to another country if they did not listen, but to no avail. The Controller sent announcers that were army officers, poets, and even singers of love songs, but still they would not listen."

Ian interjected, "Perhaps they were confused by the false announcers."

"Yes," replied John, "these false announcers told lies, often obviously wrong, because their messages contradicted the written terms and conditions of travel, and also contradicted the information boards. But many believed these false announcements and left the train to Zion for good. Worse still, the passengers stopped believing the true announcements because there were so many false announcements. The passengers preferred to believe what other passengers said, rather than the truth given by the true announcers."

John continued: "One of the latter announcers, Jerry was his name, predicted the great crash, even to the exact date. He predicted that many passengers would have to get off, and go to another country by foot. He predicted that the train to Zion would take a big detour for 70 years, but eventually return to the same place. Another announcer announced a second crash, and an even longer detour, 1,880 years, but again the train would return to the same place, after collecting passengers from every country of the world, speaking every language. Much suffering was foretold for the original passengers, but eventually their sufferings would be over, complete, accomplished, and they would be recompensed. This group of passengers produced some of the most moving music and poetry ever written; honey came forth out of the carcass of this lion!

"Zech was one of the last announcers before me," John continued. "He said that the three types of crew: announcers, drivers, and cleaners, would be replaced by a new train, with a new driver, and different crew. For 400 years there were no more announcers, no new announcements, just time to consider all the past announcements that had been ignored. Then, finally, the Controller sent me to prepare the people for the new train. It was to be different, but containing many of the original features, so they needed a clear warning. They were expecting the new train to be a military train, very powerful, and just for them. In fact the new train is for all, very powerful indeed, but destined to crash before being remade, and recycled into a train that would go on forever.

"One of the new crew announced the introduction of the new train. It was a quiet affair, in a stable outside an inn, in a depot called 'The House of Bread.' A few shepherds came, and visitors from the East brought some presents. Many were fearful of the new train, they demonstrated against it, they feared it would make too much noise, and disturb their sleep. They feared the bright color would blind people as the sun reflected from its finely honed surface. They feared the new driver would not know the way to Zion. In fact, the first trip this new train took was an emergency evacuation to Coventry, with only two passengers on board, Mary and Joe, as the local authority had condemned the new train, and wanted it scrapped before it had even made its inaugural journey."

Chapter 13

The Goat Train

"LET ME TELL YOU about one of the first train drivers," said John to Ian, and his friends, as they sped through the rolling countryside, occasionally glimpsing sheep and goats enjoying the green grass, and the spring sunshine. Ian and Nick had been fascinated by what John had to say, but their two other friends, Gareth and Methedig, were getting a bit bored from just sitting and listening, so they made their excuses and left to explore the train on their own. Ian did not urge them to return quickly, something he was going to regret.

"The first train driver was a shepherd," explained John. "He looked after both sheep and goats in the arid wilderness of the Sinai Peninsula. He learnt how to feed his flock, how to lead them in the right direction, how to care for them when they were sick, and find them when they got lost. He led them beside still waters. He gave them water to drink, and he would wash them to remove all the dirt that naturally clung to their sticky coats. They learnt how to recognize his voice, and they trusted him enough to follow him wherever he led them. He loved his flock, every one of them.

"This shepherd was a bit of a fitness fanatic," continued John. "He was able to run a marathon in the desert. He was stronger than an ox, and he could catch even the most rebellious rams, and he could fight off the most ferocious of lions that used to attack the flock.

"Once a year the shepherd would go on a journey. It was the same date every year, the tenth of July. He took the two very best specimens, male goats in their prime. One he sacrificed, and burnt whole outside the camp, while the other he spared. The spared goat was called 'the scapegoat,' and it had a very important job to do. All the wrongs done by everyone in the whole country were brought to him. There were over two million families, and not one of them was perfect. Each one had confessed the things they had done wrong during the last year, and had written them down on white stones. All these white stones were then collected, and given to the shepherd. The stones formed an enormous pile. It was so big it blocked out the sun from shining on them, and retarded the growth of their crops too. There was less light so the crops struggled to grow in the shadow of this hideous pile of stones. This great darkness was going to lead to their death unless something was done.

"The solution to this was the first ever train. The shepherd loaded the stones one by one into carts. He then joined the carts together with iron couplings to form a train. It was a vast train; two million carriages, one for each family. Some carriages were full to overflowing with white stones completely covered in writing; others contained just a few stones that were nearly, but not quite, pure white. There were no empty carts in this train.

"Next, the shepherd put a wooden harness on the goat that had been spared, and connected the harness to the train of carts. The harness was made from one long piece of wood linking the goat to the train, and at 90° a second shorter piece that went on the shoulders of the goat that was tied to it. Then the shepherd gave the goat a drink from the spring of life, and said the word 'Go.' Then, very slowly but surely, the train began to move. Eventually it reached its top speed of four mph, with the shepherd walking beside the goat at the front of the train. The shepherd's job was to drive the goat in the right direction, not round and round in circles, but in a straight line out into the desert. There were no rails to guide the train then. He drove the goat train away from the camp, away from their fields, away from the people. It was tough going, and hot sweaty work. The shepherd's journey took him through a tall thicket of thorns, where he felt the thorns pierce his side and his head; he could not remove the thorns on the crown of his head, so deeply did they penetrate his skull. He was sweating blood and tears by now.

"They continued out into the lonely wilderness, where nobody ventured; as far as the east is from the west they traveled. There at last they halted, and unloaded all the stones. Here lay a vast chasm, a fault line, a hole in the earth's crust. It was even hotter here. The shepherd could see red-hot lava gently flowing below him in a vast red lake. One by one he rolled the stones into this lake, and watched them as they were consumed by the lava; they literally melted, and then sank deep into the heart of the earth. Though there were many stones, and they were cold in comparison to the lava, they did not cool this crimson lake at all. The heat of the earth was so great it could melt these two million stones each year, and still be ready to absorb many more train loads of stones from many more nations to come.

"The shepherd declared, 'It is finished!' and with that he set the goat free. The goat ran off into the desert having carried his burden to its fiery destination, accomplished his goal, and saved all the people from the shadow of the pile of stones that was making their lives intolerable, and in so doing gave them new life.

"The next day, back at the camp, new stones started arriving; a new pile of stones was forming, very small at first. They could not help it; they seemed programmed to do wrong things. They realized how painful and burdensome this wrongdoing was and wanted to be free of their burden, so they started bringing the stones to the place where they would be taken away by the next train, in a year's time.

"Within a month this pile was ten meters high, and within twelve months it had once again become intolerable, a great blot on the landscape. So, once again the shepherd had to find another pair of goats, and continue to have faith that a single scapegoat could pull this great train full of stones through the desert into the lava lake once more. He had to believe that this dark shadow could be removed, and that the sun would shine once again to produce the grapes, oranges, wheat, barley, and grass, over the next season, so they could make their wine, bread, and orange juice, as well as feed their flocks, which would give them meat to eat, and clothes to wear, for the year ahead.

"This pattern repeated itself year-on-year for many years, until one year the shepherd who was due to drive the train was not in his place on the 10th of July. He had met a girl from the next city, and had been invited to a party that coincided with the train's departure time. The pile of stones had built up as usual, in fact it seemed even taller than usual, as if it might topple over, and kill someone at any moment.

"The shepherd's girl-friend was so excited that he was coming to see her. She said it didn't really matter about the pile of stones, her city had lots of piles of stones going back decades, even centuries in some cases, and anyway couldn't he drive his train next week after the party. So the shepherd left his sheep, his goats, his train, his city, and all the people he was rostered to serve, and arrived in E-Dom, where his girlfriend lived. He had a great time there; he forgot all about his people, and just enjoyed the moment. One night after a particularly close encounter, and after consuming several glasses of E-Dom's excellent wine, he asked her to marry him. She said, 'Yes,' on condition that he moved to E-Dom, and gave up his job as a train driver. He was reluctant to give up his job, that he knew was so important for his people, but love, or was it lust, for this most attractive young girl blinded his eyes, his mind, and his heart. He reasoned that he had done his bit for the company by now, and so he stayed in E-Dom and gave up his job of removing the white stones.

"The next year, the pile was twice as high, the year after just over three times as high, and after four years it was five times as high. The inhabitants were getting used to it; they started making buildings from the stones, places where they rejoiced in all the wrong that was written on the stones. These things were still called 'wicked,' but for most people the word 'wicked' had come to mean cool. They constructed brothels, clinics for killing their children before they were born, and concentration camps to contain and exterminate all those who spoke out against their wickedness.

"A few goats survived and one or two shepherds tried to look after them, but the job of moving this vast edifice of stones was overwhelming, and it just got bigger and bigger, until one day a new shepherd was born; a good shepherd. He was born in a stable in a bakery, and after a brief period as an asylum seeker in a foreign land, he grew up as a carpenter. He used his carpentry skills to remake the harness that was previously used to tie the scapegoat to the train of carts filled with the white stones. He then attached one end of this wooden cross-shaped device to the front of the train, and the other end was attached to his own body with nails.

"He took all the white stones himself, and filled up all the empty, waiting carts. He made a new train: it had two separate parts, the front was a passenger train that was free for anyone to travel on, and the rear was the endless train of carts filled with stones. However, before putting the stones in the carts, he wiped away every word written on the white stones with his own blood, so they became beautiful pink stones, a memorial to his work. The memory of what had been written on the stones was completely removed. He then took his place at the head of the train by being nailed to the wooden cross-shaped harness, and set off—for Zion. He invites all who want to board this train to offload their burden of white stones, and take their place in one of the specially reserved passenger cars at the front of the train. There is plenty of room for all; he made sure of that.

"Sadly, many still prefer to build their own edifices from their white stones, and can't quite believe that there is a train that will take away their stones, and transport their souls to the great city paved with gold that is called Zion."

And with that John ended his discourse. Ian and Nick pondered this tale for some time, wondering about their own white stones, the new train driver, and the awful pile of stones. Ian thought about all his old friends back in Talybont, the stonewalls there, the barns built from white-washed stones, and the great dark shadow cast by all those buildings that prevented even the grass from growing to the north of them. As a boy he had often wondered why there were no flowers there, now he knew.

"That was a strange beginning," said Nick to Ian.

"Indeed," agreed Ian, still contemplating this mysterious tale. Then breaking into Ian's train of thought, Nick asked, "Where are the others?" Gareth and Methedig had been gone some time.

"No idea," said Ian. He had been so enthralled by John's tale that he had forgotten all about his other two friends.

"Shall I continue?" asked John.

"Oh yes," said Ian.

Chapter 14

Mind the Gap

JOHN THEN RECOUNTED THE most famous announcement of all: "*Mind the gap.*"

"There was a gap between the platform and the train to Zion, which had to be bridged to get onto the train. The gap was too wide for any human to step over it unaided. Many had tried, and fallen down the gap. The gap was full of all the failings of mankind; arrogance, self-importance, pride, independence, self-pity, fear, negative speaking, hatred, to name but a few.

"The very first rail systems were designed with no gap between the rails and the platform, and passengers could come and go as they pleased with ease. It was perfectly straight, so did not need a gap. However, one day a passenger called Adam wanted to re-design the train, he felt he could do a better job. Or was it his wife who had the idea? Anyway a new train was created that could not travel on the straight and narrow line of Eden, and had to be relocated. It was able to negotiate bends, it could go anywhere, but it was spoilt, prone to rust, and worst of all, had this massive gap between the train and the platform which prevented passengers from getting on un-aided. A few did manage to get on with the help of the Controller; Ab, Issi, Jake, Moshe, Elias, Caleb, and Josh were the names of some who managed to get on the train."

"I think I may have met some of these on the train already," interjected Ian, pleased to be able to relate to John's story. Nick was rather puzzled, as he thought John had already told the tale of the first rail system, or perhaps it was the first train. Or was it the first driver? He could not quite remember.

Then John continued; "So that is why we have to say, '*Mind the gap*,' even today.

"But anyone can get on the train if they ask for help. The new crew member will be delighted to help anyone who wants to get on the train to Zion. So, as long as you are prepared to let go, and trust him, he will bridge the gap for you. The new driver built a unique bridge mechanism himself, which allows anyone who asks to bridge this gap and board the train; old, young, heavy, light, black, white, slave or free, Jew or gentile.

"It was a very costly business however to build this special bridge over the gap. A cross-shaped bridge was needed. Some say it is made of gold, others say it is made from wood from the tree of knowledge; others say it is made from the new driver's own flesh and blood.

"Some of the older announcers had also spoken of this gap, and how it would be bridged. Yesha Yahu said: 'But your iniquities have made a separation between you and your God . . . All of us like sheep have gone astray. Each of us has turned to his own way; but the LORD has caused the iniquity of us all to fall on Him . . . He Himself bore the sin of many, and interceded for the transgressors.'[9]

"One of the earliest attempts to bridge this gap resulted in disaster. It happened in Iraq, many many years ago. There had been a bit of a downpour, and the earth had only just dried out. The people there said, 'Come, let us build for ourselves a city, and a tower whose top will reach into heaven, and let us make for ourselves a name.'[10] They were proud of what they had built, but the Controller knew that their efforts would never be enough, their tower could never be tall enough to reach the sky, let alone heaven, so he scattered them over the face of the earth, hoping they would realize the futility of their efforts.

"During the millennia that followed, many have tried to bridge this gap with their own efforts, whole religions have been created with this in mind. People have tried to build a bridge with prayers, even constructing machines that pray prayers for them. Others have chosen to put their faith in five sturdy looking pillars—reciting a creed, fasting, giving to the poor, praying every day towards a sacred place, and going on pilgrimage to a place in the desert. Others have thought that witnessing on the streets, or door-to-door, to 'Jehovah' will be enough, but it isn't. Many think that going to an old building with a pointed tower once a week, and trying to do good to everybody is enough to bridge this gap, but it isn't. All have fallen short when they try to mind the gap through their own efforts.

"If we say we have no sin we are deluding ourselves. It is blood that cleanses from sin. Many are put off by the thought of blood and of sacrifice. But the ticket to ride on the train to Zion is printed with blood, human blood; divine blood.

"This ancient people had an inkling, a picture, a shadow of this vital truth. They knew they did things wrong and offended the Controller. They employed special people to offer sacrifices of blood on their behalf, once a year on the Day of Atonement, and at other times when they knew they had done wrong. They had a special tent for the purpose, and later a special building, a magnificent temple, built by Davidson, whose mother was Beth Sheba. This temple was sited on a little hill where their ancestor Ab had shown he was prepared to sacrifice his own dear son. But even that was not enough to bridge the gap. It was just a shadow of what was to come.

"Davidson's father realized this even before the special building was built. In one of his famous songs he wrote; 'Sacrifice and offering You did not desire; my ears You have opened. Burnt offering and sin offering You did not require.'[11] About 800 years later this song was still being sung, and finally people realized what it meant. The sacrifice of an animal cannot take away sin and bridge the gap, but there is one sacrifice that can, and does, bridge the gap, once and for all; this is the sacrifice of God's own Son, the Rescuer Messiah, who died in our place, instead of us, taking the required consequences of our sin on Himself. He was separated from His Father, as the horror of the evil actions of the whole world fell on his back at the cross, placed just a short distance from where the special building had been built. This Rescuer Messiah was perfect, He loved us so much, that He was prepared to give up His own life, so that we might live. And it worked. His sacrifice *was* enough to make a way for all of us to cross over this gap. We were all bought with this price, His blood. We were redeemed. And because He did not deserve death, death could not hold him, so He rose from the dead, and appeared to many eye witnesses, who wrote down their account recording the evidence, which anybody can examine today.

> *Christ died in our place,*
> *but God raised Him to life again,*
> *and He appeared to many people, some of whom wrote down what they saw,*
> *so that we too might believe, and be reconciled with God;*
> *and thus be at peace with God*
> *forever.*[12]

"This is good news for everybody.

"However, it is possible to remain on the platform, even though you know all about the gap, and the bridge over the gap made from the flesh and blood of Christ. You can sit on a comfortable bench on the platform watching all the passengers getting on the train, looking at the ramp being extended over the gap onto the train, calculating if it will take your weight or not, pondering, discussing, procrastinating forever, until death do us part. You can even believe that the bridge over the gap exists, and will take your weight, and still do nothing about it.

"Somebody called James Mercy-Over-Judgment had quite a lot to say about this. He said, 'faith without works is dead.'[13] Faith is like an undeveloped x-ray, an unborn child, a virtual particle, until it produces action. The action demonstrates that the faith was real, and not just wishful thinking. So the person with true faith will not continue to sit on the comfortable bench, or on the fence, but will get up, and walk up to the gap, put his full weight onto the bridge over the gap, and enter the train through the open door.

"Many announcers have announced, 'Mind the gap,' in many ways, and in many different countries, over many centuries. Ambassador Tarsus said, 'Take heed lest you fall,' in a letter to his friends in Corinth. Jude Thaddaeus ended his letter with this wonderful crescendo: 'Now to Him who is able to keep you from stumbling, and to make you stand in the presence of His glory blameless with great joy, to the only God our Savior, through Jesus Christ our Lord, be glory, majesty, dominion and authority, before all time and now and forever. Amen.'[14]

"The people of Ephesus in Turkey received a letter from Ambassador Tarsus, that went something like this: 'by grace you have been saved through faith and that not of yourselves, it is the gift of God not as a result of your own efforts so that no one should be able to boast before almighty God.'"

This reminded Nick of the time he was saved from a train crash on the way to a trainspotters convention, and how he was brought back to Aberystwyth to catch the train to Zion.

At this point Gareth burst into the carriage laughing loudly at a joke Methedig had just told him. They had not heard a word John had said.

Ian, however, remembered the time when his cousin Dafydd visited his cottage back in Wales and told him how he had been healed after hearing a man called John Newton from Wapping speak, and sing this hymn which he had composed:

A Ticket to Zion

Amazing grace! How sweet the sound
That saved a wretch like me!
I once was lost, but now am found;
Was blind, but now I see.

'Twas grace that taught my heart to fear,
And grace my fears relieved;
How precious did that grace appear
The hour I first believed

Through many dangers, toils and snares,
I have already come;
Tis grace hath brought me safe thus far,
And grace will lead me home.

The Lord has promised good to me,
His Word my hope secures;
He will my Shield and Portion be,
As long as life endures.

Yea, when this flesh and heart shall fail
And mortal life shall cease,
I shall possess, within the veil,
A life of joy and peace.

The earth shall soon dissolve like snow,
The sun forbear to shine;
But God, who called me here below,
Will be forever mine.

When we've been there ten thousand years,
Bright shining as the sun,
We've no less days to sing God's praise
Than when we'd first begun.[15]

Ian now realized that he had received this grace for himself, confessed that he had been a wretch, and had believed and trusted in Christ to save him from falling into the great gap that is the pit of death and sin. Ian now had the "blessed assurance" that he was on the right train. He had asked for help to bridge the great gap between the platform and the train, and he had accepted the offer of the free ticket to Zion, which was his most prized possession. He wanted to mark the occasion in some way.

The Rail Company had an arrangement to divert the train to Zion to a place where there was plenty of water whenever someone on the train had this realization, and wanted to celebrate it publically. If it was in summer, the train often went to the seaside, in winter to a swimming pool. Alternatively, some buildings had pools made especially for such occasions. As it was spring when Ian had this realization, he asked if the train could go to one of these special pools, so the train to Zion finally departed from London for this important service.

Ian invited all his friends from Talybont, as well as all those already on the train to Zion, to this special event. Nick, Gareth, and Methedig were there, and a good number of other people from the train to Zion he didn't know, but none of his friends from Talybont came. He publically declared that because the Controller loved us all so much He sent His own son to die in our place. He proclaimed that the Controller made Him alive again, that He appeared to many people after His death (demonstrating His power), and that what He said was true. Then to the astonishment of all those watching Ian was plunged into the pool, and held underwater. Ian did not drown though; he was raised up again (rather like the Controller's son had been), and then Ian sang as he had never sung before, with all his heart, and tears ran down his face just like those coal miners a hundred years ago in the Welsh revival. He was full of joy and peace, looking forward, with renewed joy and great anticipation, to the rest of the journey to Zion.

So the train moved on, with Ian in high spirits, through sunny glades and bright shining lakes, slowly winding its way through the land ever closer to Zion.

After a good few hours, Ian realized he hadn't eaten anything for ages. So taken was he with John's discourse that he had completely forgotten about food. So he left his seat, and his three friends, in search of the restaurant car, or at least a kiosk selling sandwiches and tea. On his way there he was surprised by joy; a sudden jolt of great joy, most unexpected, seemed to land on him like a dove landing on a dovecote. Then he bumped into Dafydd!

"Dafydd, is that you, is that really you?"

"Yes," replied Dafydd, with such a broad smile on his face he could hardly talk. "Dafydd, thank you so much for telling me the good news about the free ticket to Zion."

"It was a pleasure," said Dafydd.

"It is so good to see you again," said Ian, "you must tell me all about what you have been up to, where you have been, and who you have met."

"OK, but let's do that over a meal, I'm quite ready for supper, aren't you?"

"Oh yes," said Ian.

So, reunited like long lost friends, the two of them sat down to have their supper. And what a supper it was! It was like the first meal in the Promised Land after forty years in the wilderness; there were pomegranates as big as footballs, a cluster of grapes so enormous it took two waiters to bring it in, and fresh figs like Ian had never tasted before (he was used to those hard blocks of dried figs you buy in the supermarket). There was milk flowing with honey, wine from Lebanon, and water from the upper springs that Caleb had given to his daughter. All was served in golden bowls and crystal glasses. Ian felt that he had been brought into a royal banqueting hall, with a great banner hanging over him which proclaimed the love of the one who had prepared all this for him (and for all who take their seat at this table).

So Dafydd began his story.

"After I left you in Talybont, I caught a train to India, and then a bus to Bhutan. To get there I had to go through a war zone in the Middle East. My seven older brothers were soldiers fighting in the war against the Palestinians. My parents had given me ten different cheeses from their farm to take to my brothers. I had left my sister in charge of the farm while I was away. After a long journey, I arrived at the front line. I could smell the fear. Everybody seemed afraid of the Palestinians. They had intimidated their enemy for forty days. It was a standoff. A big battle seemed imminent. Then a message came from the Palestinians: 'Choose a man from your ranks, and come, let us settle this in a dual, one versus one. That way only one person will die rather than half of our two armies.' This seemed logical, the only problem was that the one the Palestinians had chosen was an Olympic wrestling champion, who had also once played against the All Blacks, and won. All seven of my brothers were busy looking the other way, trying not to be seen by the commander as he looked for a volunteer, but also trying not to look as frightened as they actually were. Then they spotted me.

"'What are you doing here,' they shouted at me, 'come to see the fight? Who is looking after those few sheep of yours?'

"I explained that my sister was looking after them, and that I had brought them some cheese. Then I heard about this fat lump who was intimidating the whole army. I couldn't believe nobody wanted to fight him. To me he looked very slow and ponderous; I knew I could beat him. Somebody overheard what I had said, and reported it to the commander, who summoned me in to see him. Well, to cut a long story short, I ended up being the one chosen for the dual!

"They gave me this heavy armor-plated jacket to wear, and the latest weapons, but I didn't know how to use them, plus I could hardly move in all the kit I was wearing. So I took the whole lot off, and just went as I was. I did say a prayer though before I set off, and I took with me my catapult that I had used for years on the farm to kill rabbits before I became blind, you know the one don't you? I hadn't used it since I was healed, so I set up twelve cans on a wall, and I managed to knock them all off in twelve shots—my sight had been restored to even better than it was before! Having been blind, I had also learnt to listen very attentively, so I knew if I hid half way down the hill behind an oak tree, I would hear him coming before he could see me. I managed to get to my tree, where I hid, then loaded up my catapult, and zingggg, straight on his forehead; he was down in one.

"And that is how we defeated the Palestinians who were threatening to kill all my brothers. I was quite the hero after that, they even wrote a song about the fight, but the commander was less pleased when the song went viral—I think he was a bit jealous of me, but it was only because I prayed and trusted God, that I had won."

"That was quite an adventure, Dafydd," Ian said, "I didn't know you had it in you!"

"It was nothing really," said Dafydd.

"What happened next?" Ian asked.

"Well," said Dafydd, "the commander made me second in command of the unit. But we didn't really get on. He became more and more jealous of my success on the battlefield, with my songs, and with the young ladies! His jealousy seemed to eat away at his soul; he became violent towards me, some kind of mental disorder I think. Several times he tried to kill me. But I just kept clear, and tried to do my job the best I could. Anyway, eventually it got too hot for me, and I escaped. I had to live in a cave, and steal bread from a church to get by. After a couple of years on the run, I heard that the commander and his son had been killed in a terrorist attack. I was gutted. He was the one who had given me my chance, and now he was dead. They offered me the post of commander, and this chap Sam persuaded me to take it. I fought more battles, and eventually all the enemies seemed to fade away, and we had peace.

"Then I made a big mistake. I had stayed home while the army was out fighting, and I spotted this girl Beth sunbathing without anything on at all. I fell for her, even though she had just got married to this fantastic guy. I was besotted. I arranged for her new husband to be sent to the most dangerous unit in the army. He never came back, and after a suitable interval I married the girl, and we had a son. Instead of feeling happy with her, I felt guilty. Nathan, one of my friends, wrote a little poem about our relationship, and the death of her first husband. I then realized how bad I had been.

"My other son rebelled, and made my life hell. I ended up escaping to where that first battle with the Palestinians was. I even pretended to be mad.

"Anyway, eventually I returned, and set about building a brand new train station. It was to be the most magnificent station ever built. However, I never got to build it. I did make all the preparations for it, I got the exact design sorted, the site ready, and all the materials; it took years. The son

I had with Beth Sheba, is going to build it after I die. So with that project completed as far as I could, I decided to continue my journey by train, and then I bumped into you again!"

"Wonder of Wonders!" Ian said. "Wow, that was quite an adventure."

Ian then recounted how he had picked up his ticket to Zion, overcome the temptations to go another way, how he had seen the wrong train pass by, how he had encouraged Nick, Gareth, and Methedig to join him on the train to Zion, and how had heard about the old train crew before the current driver had taken charge. He also told Dafydd how he was surprised by joy when he had seen him again, and how his heart was burning within him whenever he was hearing about events on the train to Zion.

Chapter 15

Cleaners and Drivers

Due to his reunion with Dafydd, and John's fascinating tales, Ian had rather ignored his two friends Gareth and Methedig. Ian thought he heard someone say it was time to return to his two friends, but he ignored it. Instead Ian was keen to return to John so he could hear more wonderful stories. Ian still had questions burning in his heart; who ran the rail system, who were the train crew, and how could he help? When Ian had met John earlier, he had learnt something about the announcers, but what about the rest of the crew? It was now time, he felt, to ask about the cleaners and the drivers. Dafydd was always interested to discuss train history, so when John came to the restaurant car they invited him to join them. They remained at their table in the restaurant car long after the dishes had been cleared away. They urged John to tell them all about the cleaners and the drivers. John was more than happy to oblige.

"The cleaners were those who removed the rubbish created by the passengers in the train. Every day they cleaned it, but every day it got dirty again. The toilets were the worst. They were smelly, unhealthy, and often got blocked. It was the cleaner's job to unblock the toilets. The toilets also had a rather disgusting feature, disgusting for people near the train, because they discharged their contents directly onto the track. This put off many people from taking the train to Zion. There were instructions not to flush at stations, where people were waiting to get on, but these instructions were often ignored. So, many people let the train to Zion pass them by, hoping for a nicer train, but there is only one train to Zion. The train to Zion would actually be very clean, and not smelly at all, if it were not for the passengers! Because of the discharge from the passenger toilets, the track workers learnt to turn their backs whenever the train to Zion approaches.

"The cleaners wore special clothes, so everyone knew they were cleaners. The clothes were designed to protect them from the filth, but some wore the uniform rather as a badge of honor, proudly declaring how much better they were than the passengers, because of all the sacrifices they had made.

"Many years ago, the Controller had appointed an ex-murderer called Moshe, to drive the train out of a siding where it had become stuck. Moshe was the one who had written the first edition of the terms and conditions for the sale of tickets to Zion. It was this Moshe who appointed the first cleaner, giving detailed instructions about exactly how to clean the train, how often, and the appropriate tools for the job.

"However, when the new train came, there was no need for cleaners anymore. The new train was self-cleaning. It was cleaned once and for all by the new crew member. Now the toilets never get blocked, they smell of red roses, and their cleansing water never ceases to flow. The discharges are now stored in a special container, and turned into fertilizer to grow the roses and lilies of the valley that provide the perfume for the toilets.

"Despite this new train, the track workers still turn their backs on the train to Zion, even 2,000 years later. Most have forgotten why they do this. One or two over the years have had the courage to overcome this tradition, and take a look, and have been rewarded with the sight of a beautiful gleaming train, brighter than gold, bathed in sunshine, and giving off a wonderful aroma. However, most still recall the old stories of the bad smell of the old train, and do not believe the good news that the train is renewed, and ready and able to take anyone on a wonderful journey to Zion free of charge.

"Finally the drivers . . ." continued John, checking that Ian and Dafydd, were still keen to hear his tale, which they most certainly were, ". . . they used to drive the train to Zion before the Controller's son came. In those days all the trains had drivers, but not anyone could be a driver, you had to be in the union, you had to have been elected, or be part of a family of drivers. Some trains were hijacked by uncertified drivers who murdered the driver (and often those next in line too).

"In those days, a beautiful train set out on its way to Zion, driven by a driver called David, who was the third driver ever to drive the train to Zion. His son finished making the train but David's grandson was not kind, and although he was given a chance to drive the train, he acted harshly towards the passengers, and there was a revolt. The train was de-coupled; 5/6th of it was formed into a new train with a different driver, and 1/6th remained as the original train. It was this smaller train that continued to have drivers from David's family, for fourteen generations in fact, ending with the Controller's son."

Dafydd was a common name in the Welsh valleys, and Ian had not realized that David was the English version of Dafydd, and that his cousin Dafydd was in fact a descendant of the very same David that was the third ever driver of the train to Zion (after Ben Kish and Ish-bosheth).

"That is my family!" said Dafydd to the astonishment of both John and Ian. "But do continue," insisted Dafydd, so John recommenced his tale.

"The longer part of the train to Zion took a wrong turn. One after another its drivers took the train in the wrong direction. They wanted the train to Zion to be like all the other trains. The train to Zion was a Special, it was meant to show all the other trains how a train service should be run, but the drivers of the long part of the train to Zion turned it into a train like any other; they refurbished it, they removed the steam engine, replacing it with a dirty diesel engine, as it was more efficient, they repainted it to look like all the other trains, and they sacked all the old guards because they wanted the driver to be solely responsible for opening and shutting the train doors. They took on crew from the other train companies. They ignored the instructions from the Controller. In those days there were frequent accidents, many drivers were killed, and many passengers died because the train was not maintained as it should have been, nor cleaned properly to prevent the spread of deadly viruses.

"Many announcements were made by the true announcers about the dire state of the rail system in those days, but most of the time nobody took any notice. Fatigue cracks were growing in the rails. The train itself was starting to look rusty too—it was originally made of gold, silver, and brass so that it would not rust, but generations of drivers had replaced this with steel because they thought it was stronger, which it was, but they forgot that steel contains iron, which eventually rusts away.

"The drivers had abandoned the depot which was purpose-built for the train to Zion, and erected their own buildings. These buildings looked more like hotels than places to care for trains. They had completely foreign protocols, they paid no attention to the Controller's instructions, the drivers just pleased themselves, took control of fares policy, put up the price of tickets so they could fund their lavish lifestyle, and got rid of all the other crew members. Right next to these new depots they built 'red light districts.'

Most thought they were called red light districts because of the red signals that halted the trains at the depots, but in fact the red lights were from bedrooms of ladies of the night, the oldest profession in the world, where the drivers often used to spend the night away from their wives, pretending they needed to be near their train to make an early start in the morning.

"They also installed new switches (or 'points' as some call them) at the top of all the hills in the land. These were manufactured by another train company, and they were designed to redirect the trains off in the wrong direction. So, instead of continuing on the straight and narrow track towards Zion, many trains veered off course downhill into sidings where there wasn't even a buffer to halt the train before it crashed into the town.

"The drivers were continually told to remove these switches on the top of the hills, but somehow they never did. So in those days progress to Zion was not at all easy.

"The drivers' instruction manual said they were to incline their ear to listen at all times to the Controller, and to what the announcers said, but most drivers had bought mobiles with headphones, so that they could listen to their favorite music or the football while driving. They were not interested in hearing from the Controller, each driver thought they knew best, and did not need anyone telling them what to do.

"All cabs had a copy of the Controller's instruction manual, but most of the drivers then did not bother to read it. They thought it was full of fairy stories for kids, not realizing it contained vital information for driving the train to Zion. So most copies were hidden away in a corner, used to eat sandwiches from, or the pages used to light up, or even used as toilet paper if they were caught short.

"There were nevertheless one or two exceptions. One driver called Jos, who was only eight years old, a record, when he started driving a train, found a copy of the Controller's instructions in his cab. One night he stayed up all night and read them from cover to cover by torch light. He was appalled. He realized the drivers before him had been driving their trains in completely the wrong way.

"So he used the income from ticket sales to restore the original depot, he banned mobile phones from all cabs, and inclined his ear to listen to what the Controller had to say to him, and about how to run the rail service. Jos was one of the most humble tenderhearted drivers ever. The train services ran on time, there were no strikes, the toilets were clean, and the people loved the music he played during the journeys. He even removed the faulty switches/points on the hill tops, including the original one installed by Davidson.

"But this golden era did not last. The driver to take over from Jos, his son no less, undid all the good he had done, and the rail service reverted back to what it was before, if not worse. Some drivers had even taken it upon themselves to offer an abortion service to dispose of the many unwanted babies from the red light district. The drivers used to take the newly born babies up to the top of the highest hill on the route and throw them out of the cab as they were speeding down the other side of the hill in the wrong direction. They thought it was a driver's responsibility to do this, to deal with the problem of unwanted children. This was the last straw for the Controller. After this, he turned up the volume on the tannoy, and sent his best announcers out to give a final warning, to turn round, to listen to him, and to read *his* instructions. But when they did not heed even this warning, he sent in the bulldozers. A new transport company arrived, which did not care about trains at all—it was a car company. They built tarmac roads for their horseless carriages where there had been but muddy tracks before, and eventually massive four-lane highways were built throughout the country. The rail lines were dismantled, the rolling stock set on fire, and the stations converted to highway service areas. The drivers were all unemployed now. Many left the country to live out their remaining days on the Costa Brava, but they were not happy there—they were made to drive trains, not to lie on the beach.

"All the treasures were parceled off to museums. The original bell, the silver whistle, and even an entire steam engine were rescued, but only to stand idle in a dusty old museum that few took the trouble to visit.

"For seventy years there was no rail system at all, but eventually a rail transport system of sorts was built, but it was nothing like the original. Those who remained, who remembered the original, wept when they saw the tiny little utilitarian trains mostly used by tourists. They wept over the roads that had largely replaced the rail system that Davidson had built.

"There were no more drivers for 400 years.

"Then when the time was ready, the Controller sent his son, his only son, to be the next train driver. Most people did not recognize Him. Many had completely forgotten what a train looked like. Others had been waiting for a renaissance of rail travel, but when the Controller's son came they ridiculed him, threw stones at him, and said terrible things about him because he looked like a servant and they were expecting a king. They thought he was born in Wapping—nothing good would ever come from Wapping—whereas the new train driver they were expecting, was to come from the House of Bread.

"But the Controller's son did re-establish the rail system. He rebuilt the lines, without the faulty switches/points this time. He installed a completely different signaling system, manufactured by the Controller's brother. He issued a supplementary guidance appendix to the old instruction manual, complete with color pictures and links to sound tracks, which was much easier to understand, but still true to the original. He taught the principles of rail travel like no one before him; everyone was amazed when they heard him speak. He mended everything that was brought to him, so great crowds used to assemble just to catch a glimpse of him. He fed five thousand people with a boy's lunch once. Another time, he rescued a wedding party when they had run out of wine. Twelve new train crew were trained by him, they were not drivers in the traditional sense though. He was now the driver of the train to Zion, who was going to be with them always. The old-style drivers were no longer needed. Instead he established a new train crew which including pioneers who were sent out to establish new lines, and two types of announcers: one type for those already on the train to Zion, and a second group who were to invite new passengers on board and give out the free tickets to everyone. He also appointed train-care officers and teachers, to take care of the growing number of passengers. The new train crew were to serve the passengers who would not just sit in their seats all day, but the passengers themselves were to invite new passengers to come on board until every seat on the train to Zion was taken.

"The main purpose for the Controller sending his son, was not in fact to be a new train driver, or to renew the rails. Rail travel had been destroyed by people from all over the world rebelling against the Controller and trying to build their own transport system. This hatred of trains had to be quashed. The only way the Controller had to rescue people was for his own dear son to accept the punishment due to them. The son paid the price due for all the damage done.

"The Controller loved the world so much that he sent his own dear son, so that whoever believes in him should not die but have everlasting life. The new rail system was built on faith, not works; faith in the Controller's son, and in what he had accomplished. He gave his very life for this, so that it would be open to all, and free to all. He promised anyone who wanted to board the train that he would make sure they reached Zion as long as they stayed on the train."

Ian was convinced he would stay on the train to Zion until the end, but he was less sure about his friends. Nick had stayed with him to hear about the train crew, but where were his other two friends Gareth and Methedig? Abandoned by Ian and Dafydd, they had wandered off and had started to look at the other trains. Gareth was missing his rugby and Methedig had settled for living the rest of his life disabled; he did not have the faith to get out of his wheelchair and enjoy the train as much as everyone else. So they had said goodbye to Nick, and got off the train at Saint Margaret's station, next to Twickenham, where there was a nice home for disabled people, frequent rugby matches for Gareth to watch, and plenty of opportunities for adventures on other trains. They didn't even say goodbye to Ian.

Chapter 16

The Wrong Train

IAN HAD NOT REALIZED that his other friends, Gareth and Methedig had not returned to the train to Zion. Though Ian searched earnestly for Gareth and Methedig for the rest of his time on the train, he never found them. This was a sadness Ian carried with him for the rest of his journey.

Then just across the platform another train pulled in at the same time. The destination written on the front of this train was not all that distinct, but it seemed to say, "Sion." There was quite a commotion on the platform, much discussion about where this other train was actually heading. It was more modern, had very smart seats, black curtains, and lamps with red lampshades. The aroma from the restaurant car was most inviting; a red lamb curry most likely. Several on the platform looked hungry and thirsty, and weren't too bothered if the train was heading for Zion, Sion, Sin, Son, Zon, or wherever, and just got on. Others looked more carefully. The "o" in Sion seemed to have been added later for some reason. There was a debate between two old rather scholarly looking men wearing prayer shawls; one was saying Zion and Sion were one and the same, the other was adamant that they were different places altogether.

About 90% of the people waiting on the platform got onto the train to Sion. Quite a few on the train to Zion decided that the Sion train looked a better bet, and changed trains where they found a much more comfortable seat. The train to Sion looked much bigger, faster, and superior; its passengers also seemed to look down on those on the train to Zion.

Both trains set off at the same time, so those on each train could see what was happening on the other train, but there was no way now to pass from one train to the other. The trains started on parallel tracks. Looking into the train to Sion you could just about make out some curious features. In one carriage there seemed to be human skulls attached to the inside of the doors to frighten people who might be thinking of leaving the train. There seemed to be instructions in large lettering saying something like: "Anyone who leaves this train will be killed, honor will require that his own family spill his or her blood." Another seemed to say: "The Management has a policy of tolerance; anyone who submits to enter this carriage will be welcomed as part of the brotherhood. The management also tolerates other passengers from other trains, as long as they are not on our tracks. Passengers to Zion are tolerated on this train on condition that they do not speak of Zion and they must pay a special tax of £666 to stay. No alcohol is to be consumed in this carriage." This carriage seemed to be full of men, whereas the next carriage seemed to be only for women, all dressed in black robes.

The carriage at the front of this train was quite different. It was full of academics, film stars, and sports personalities. They were so proud to be at the front of the train. They were so full of their own achievements they had not humbled themselves to consider if they were on the right train or not. The train to Sion had been good to them, why should they even think about a train to Zion? They had all been offered a free ticket for the train to Zion, but preferred their expensive first class carriage at the front of the train to Sion (or was its destination Sin, they did not really care where they were going).

Another part of the train was full of people having a party—loud music, dancing, and drinking, plus young girls being molested; knives sharpened for a fight; they obviously hadn't seen the "no alcohol" sign, or if they had they didn't care. The destination written on the outside of these cars seemed to be "*Si n*". But those inside couldn't see the sign.

Many of those on the train had taken leaflets from the waiting room, before the great hailstorm hit. Eighteen of the twenty leaflets were on this train.

After a few miles the train to Zion carried straight on, but the other train followed a line curving slowly off to the right, eventually disappearing out of sight in the opposite direction. Ian never saw this train again, nor any of its passengers.

Chapter 17

The First Train

IAN WAS FEELING SICK at the remembrance of all those people stuck on the wrong train, so he hurried to the toilet, along with several others who had also been disturbed by the sight of the other train. On returning to his carriage, he was intrigued by a conversation about the first ever train, between three men who were still wearing their anoraks, even though it was summer now, and nice and warm in the train to Zion. Matthieu, James, and Trevor were their names. Ian knew this because each wore a name badge, as if they had just returned from some kind of conference. To Ian, Matthieu looked like a typical British tax collector, but when he spoke, he had a kindly French accent. Ian couldn't place exactly where he was from, Belgium perhaps. James wore a tweed jacket with leather patches on the elbows, and there was no doubt from his accent that he originated from Birmingham. So instead of taking his normal seat, Ian settled down in an empty seat within earshot of these strangers that were about to become his friends.

"When would you say the first train was invented?" James asked Matthieu.

"2nd July 1698," Matthieu replied swiftly. He had obviously thought about this question before and was ready with his answer.

"What! That can't be right. Surely it was 27th September 1825[16] at Stockton," replied James.

"No it was 13th February 1804 in Merthyr," interjected a voice that Ian recognized as coming from the Welsh Valleys. This was Trevor.

Ian was fascinated to find out who was right, so he moved closer. He sat in the seat in the aisle right next to them so he could hear as clearly as possible why these three men had such different views about the origin of the first train.

"Why do you say 1698?" James and Trevor asked Matthieu in unison.

"Well that was when Thomas Savery patented the first steam engine; a new invention for raising of water, and occasioning motion to all sorts of mill work by the impellent force of fire, which will be of great use and advantage for draining mines, serving towns with water, and for the working of all sorts of mills where they have not the benefit of water nor constant winds."

"But that was only an *idea*. OK he had faith that an engine powered by steam could do good works like pumping water for people to drink, or to stop mines getting filled with water, or to power mills to grind grain, but he did not actually build one. Plus it did not travel on rails. In fact it did not even move at all; it only transported water, not goods or people. It must have been 1804," argued Trevor.

"Why so?" James and Matthieu retorted.

"Well, that was when Richard Trevithick built Pen-y-Darren, which pulled the first ever train of carriages on the Merthyr Tramway. They carried ten tons of iron over nine miles at five miles an hour with five wagons coupled together. It was watched by seventy people, who jumped on board because they were so impressed with the spectacle. Thus it was not only the first freight train but also the first passenger train!" announced Trevor proudly.

"No, no that wasn't a proper train," laughed Matthieu. "The first proper train was opened on 27th September 1825. It followed the first Rail Act 1821, when Parliament approved the first rail system, and King George IV signed the Act. As a result George Stevenson built a 26-mile rail line between Stockton and Darlington, a steam engine locomotive, thirty-five freight wagons, and a passenger carriage. This was surely the first proper rail service transporting goods and people."

Just then the three of them noticed Ian listening intently to their conversation, and turned to him.

"What do you think?" they asked Ian.

Ian had only intended to listen to them, but he thought it an honor to be asked his opinion by three such eminent rail experts.

Ian considered their arguments; "Thomas Savery had faith that his steam engine could pump water; it was indeed his mind that first conceived the idea of a steam engine transporting something (water). However, his faith alone did not lead to works; he needed to team up with Thomas

Newcomen before they built a real machine (actually in 1712 at Dudley Castle). Furthermore, was their faith in the right thing anyway, was their machine a true train? Surely it should move people and goods, not just water? That is the essence of a rail system," Ian explained, "plus, there wasn't a rail in sight at that time, so Mathieu can't be right."

Ian continued, "So, was the machine that Richard Trevithick built in 1804 the first true train?" Ian was inclined to agree with his countryman, Trevor, who had put forward such a convincing case (to the ears of a fellow Welshman at least) that the first train to run on rails was built in South Wales in 1804.

However, before Ian had a chance to dismiss James's 1825 date and plump for Trevor, a German gentleman called Heisenberg interrupted. He had been listening from a seat just in front of them.

"Now that *is* interesting," he commented, "I am a physics professor with a Nobel prize for my work on quantum mechanics. I am inclined to agree with Trevor and Ian. Unless a particle interacts with another particle, it does not really exist," he stated.

Neither Ian, Trevor, James, nor Matthieu, could see how this had anything to do with the origins of the train, but they let him continue nonetheless.

"Until a particle, say an electron, interacts with something, say a photon, how can we know where it is, or indeed anything about it? Before the interaction, it is just virtual, a thought, a hypothesis. A particle only has a probability of existing at a particular point in space and time, but once we detect the light, measure its energy, direction, and speed, we can then, and only then, truly know where the electron was, and deduce something about its nature."

The four of them were still puzzled.

Sighing inside at their slowness to see the relevance of his remarks Heisenberg explained: "Thomas Savery in 1698 only had an *idea*; it was not until his idea was acted upon, and his machine was built and measured, could anyone be sure it worked. This is a basic law of science. Lots of other people have had ideas about how to transport goods and people, some worked some did not; for example there was Hindenburg's hot air balloon, which was not such a good idea, as the hydrogen inside it exploded killing 35 people. So you not only have to have faith, but you have to have faith *in the right thing*, and then you also have to act on it, and turn your idea into good works, i.e. a transport system for getting people (or goods) from A to B that is better than going by horse and cart, and safe too. It is just the same with my electron and photon. It is not until I *see* the manifestation of the electron by observing the light emitted from it, that I can know that my ideas about electrons are reasonable."

The four thought they might be starting to understand, but still looked slightly puzzled. So Professor Heisenberg continued.

"Hitler had an idea that the Aryan race was superior to the Jewish race, which he wrote about in Mein Kampf in 1925, the same year that I published my ideas on quantum mechanics, but it was not until the concentration camps were liberated at the end of the war that everybody realized the full horror of his idea. Hitler placed his faith in the superiority of the Aryan race, but that was misplaced faith, as was clearly seen when his faith turned into such terrible action.

"One final example for you: in the depths of winter when a young girl placed her faith in the ice when she went skating, her faith was well-founded as she was light, and the ice was thick, and she had a wonderful time. However, the next month, when the ice was thin after days of sunshine, she fell in and drowned when the ice cracked. Her faith this time was based on a falsehood; her belief that the ice was thick enough to hold her.

"So three things are needed:

1. Faith, a belief

2. Faith that is founded on truth, rather than falsehood

3. Faith founded on truth that is tested, and found to be well-founded by putting it into practice, and measuring what actually happens.

"So with early attempts to make mobile steam engines, most were not well-founded, such as Nicolas Cugnot's 1769 self-propelled gun carriage that crashed into a wall in Paris due to inadequate steering equipment. Conversely, early ideas of transport systems were not acted on until much later, so did not come into being until the nineteenth century. The classic example of this is Leonardo da Vinci's helicopter. Though well-founded, it was not acted on, so did not really exist until the first helicopter was actually built, and flown successfully in the 1940s. So Ian and Trevor are right, in my opinion; the first train that actually moved people and goods was in 1804," concluded Professor Heisenberg.

At last Ian had got it. He had not only learnt which was the first train but also why—a truth that could explain so much, from elementary particles to which train would take him to Zion—faith without works is nothing. Ian concluded by deducing that if we believe the words of the Controller's son to get on the train to Zion, it is of no value if we "believe" the words, and then do not get on the train when it arrives—we have demonstrated that we did not really believe at all. Also, if we get on a different train, then we have put our faith in something different, and we will not find ourselves in Zion, no matter how hard we "believe" that we have got on the right train.

It was now well past lunchtime. So they all went to get something to eat. Ian chose one of the Rail Company's best sandwiches. The others decided to stay for a hot meal.

When Ian returned to his seat, he found it had been taken by a tramp, who looked like he had not washed for some time. This tramp announced to Ian that he had not eaten for a week. Instead of turfing the tramp out of his seat, Ian gave the sandwich he had bought for his lunch, and sat down next to him.

"Bless you," the tramp said.

"My pleasure," Ian replied.

The tramp had shown faith in Ian's generosity, which had been demonstrated when Ian gave the tramp his sandwich. Ian had responded to an inner voice urging him to give up his sandwich, and he had acted on this voice, believing it to be in accordance with the will of the Controller. So Ian was rewarded with a new friend, and the tramp got his lunch.

Chapter 18

The Door between the Carriages

Then still a bit hungry, and remembering his new friends had gone for lunch, Ian got up from his seat too. He went past the toilet and reached for the handle of the door at the very end of his carriage. It was very stiff, as if it had not been opened for ages, but eventually Ian managed to prize the door open and walk into the next carriage. It was beautiful, full of gold, blue, and crimson; very old fashioned, traditional, and smelling of incense. Ian could hear some faint singing. Despite his rumbling tummy he paused to listen. It sounded like the twenty-third psalm, but more authentic than he had ever heard it before.

Sitting in the seats were many old men. They looked like the old shepherds Ian had known from the hill farms of Wales where he was born. Then Ian noticed the women. They all looked identical: grey but still beautiful, fiercely loyal to their husbands, and great champions of the journey to Zion.

"Hello, I'm Ian, and you are . . . ?" Ian said in a friendly nonchalant tone.

The whole carriage looked round in astonishment. They could not remember the last time someone had come through that door in such a friendly way. All they could remember were soldiers dressed in white robes each adorned with a red cross, who had murdered many of their ancestors. (This was actually over five hundred years ago, but in their minds it seemed like yesterday.)

Then one of the oldest of the men got up from his seat, walked slowly over to Ian and stretched out his hand.

"My name is Ab" the old man said. "I am from a country far away; between two great rivers. I was called to leave my land to go to a new country but I was not told where it was. I had to walk by faith. There were no trains in those days and it was a long walk. Halfway through my journey my father died and my brother left me to return home, but I pressed on with my wife Faith. Look she is sitting just over there."

Ian looked at Faith and recognized something about her appearance that touched his heart.

"My wife and I were looking for a city with foundations that would last forever. We set out alone, just the two of us. I was afraid of who might be in this new country so I had made my wife promise that if a man ever threatened me she would give herself up to him in order to save my life by pretending to be my sister. This she did, she was so faithful to me.

"Then, a rich man with a name like mine took my wife as his wife not knowing we were married (as I had told him she was my sister, which was actually half true because she was my step-sister). It did not go well for them though, they couldn't have children. I had had no children either. When he found out that Faith was actually my wife I thought he would kill me, but instead he asked me to pray for him. This man married again, and I did pray for him as he had asked me to, and I was sorry that I had made my wife promise to do what she did. She had more faith than I had ever had. And then a miracle happened. Despite the old age of this man, he was able to have a family and lived happily ever after. Then after that, at the age of about one hundred, Faith and I finally had children! Many of the descendants of this child are here in this carriage. They too all have wives called Faith, odd isn't it?

"We are all still seeking this country that will last forever and believe with Faith that we are on the right track. We believe a city has been prepared for us. I think the city is called Zion. However, we are not there yet.

"Over the centuries, we stumbled many times, offending the Controller and his train crew, but we were always received back onto this train despite our impertinence. The biggest issue was when the Controller sent his son to our carriage. We didn't recognize him, we treated him very badly, very very badly, but enduring the bad treatment, his son saved many people in the great train crash. He went to the front of the train. The train was hurtling down a steep hill. The brakes failed. The only way to stop the train from a fatal crash was to use the emergency brake. The Controller's son knew that the momentum of all the carriages behind him would crush the driver's cab if it stopped suddenly at such a speed, but he still applied the brake. He saved all those behind him but at the cost of his own life.

"We were saved too, as were all those in the new carriages, where you have just come from. He also saved very many empty carriages. These were reserved carriages kept for all those invited to take the train to Zion, but were never filled, and they remain empty to this day, so very sad.

"Since then we have hardly ever seen anyone come through that door and when they have it has usually been with sharpened swords intent on throwing us out of this train because of the mistaken view that we killed the Controller's son. These soldiers were not really interested in the Controller's son; they just wanted this carriage for themselves and thought that retribution was due. But despite being thrown out of many carriages, our sons and daughters being killed, being blamed for the woes of the world, and finally six million of us being exterminated in a country north of here, we have survived. The Controller has now given us back the carriage we had originally and we are so grateful to be going back home.

"Over the centuries there seemed to be a dividing wall between our carriage and yours, hence I am so pleased that you have come through it to see us. We have been waiting to give you your presents. They were wrapped and ready many years ago, but they have been preserved in perfect condition for you.

"We are not all here on this train, sadly; some of us divorced our wives, and without them to guide us we got lost, however a remnant of us kept faith and, as you can see, we are still here today on the same train as you, heading for the city of Zion. We have been made into one new train; the old carriages coupled together with the new, though few fully realize this truth. Many of us can't look beyond the scars inflicted on us by the soldiers who came from your carriage, and many of you seem to think your carriages are the only ones on the train, but I want to give you this olive branch, as a sign of peace and recognition that we are fellow travelers on this train to Zion."

"Thank you," said Ian, "you are so courageous. I am so honored that you have spoken to me as you have and very pleased to shake your hand."

With excitement but tinged with apprehension Ian enquired, "Would you like to sing with me one of the songs of Zion?"

"How can we sing the songs of Zion in a foreign land?" Ab replied.

"Well," Ian persevered, "you don't have to sing then, just listen. This is a song written by John Patmos. It came to him when he was exiled on an island in the Mediterranean Sea many years ago, soon after you killed the Controller's son—I am sorry—I meant soon after the Controller's son died. I am sure it was not just your fault, we were there too, and the Rail Accident

Investigation Branch cited our faults as a significant contributing factor to the great train crash that killed him." Ian had nearly broken this new friendship with one careless phrase. However, as Ab saw that Ian was truly sorry he unblocked his ears and started to listen to John's song. Ian then played 'Twelve Gates in the City' by Stan Spottswood."

"Wow! Wonder of wonders," said Ab. "I have never heard such a wonderful song."

"These twenty four elders are your twelve grandsons plus the twelve sent out by the Controller's son," Ian explained.

Ab could hardly take it in, as tears were now flowing freely from his eyes down his beard and anointing his feet.

Eventually Ab composed himself enough to say: "Yes this is the city we are heading for. I would love to hear more but first I must give you the other presents that have been kept for you."

Ab unwrapped an old silk and gold cloth to reveal four gifts. They were:

- a scroll from the dead sea containing thirty nine "books" all about the early days of the train to Zion,

- a small crystal bottle containing the tears of the announcers,

- a gold casket containing red soil, from the holy land, mixed with the blood of Jake's children (Jake was Ab's grandson), and

- a white stone from the western wall of the Controller's house.

"Thank you so much. And I have brought you a gift too" replied Ian. Ian presented his gift; it was a set of the finest clothes you will ever see, which Ian had received earlier from a member of the train crew to give to anyone in this carriage who would appreciate it. "This is for you to wear at the feast of the ram when you get off this train and enter the city of Zion. There will be a wedding feast and angels will sing. It will last a thousand years. You can only enter the wedding feast if you have put on new clothes. Your old clothes are like rags in comparison to these new clothes. There are sets of clothes enough for all of you in this carriage, all fitting perfectly, designed by the Controller himself."

"Thank you, thank you," replied Ab most appreciatively.

"I have one final gift for you" said Ian. "It is a picture." Ian unveiled a drawing of a cross, with a star of David made out of a crown of thorns. Dripping from the cross were drops of blood, some shaped like tears, and others inverted so they looked like hearts.

"Thank you we love your gifts," said Ab. "Bless you."

The scroll that Ab had given to Ian had fallen open at the twelfth chapter of the first book where it said, "I will bless those who bless thee," so Ian knew he would indeed be blessed because he had blessed Ab, and the scroll said that the Controller would bless anyone that blessed Ab and his grandson Jake's children.

"I must return now to my own carriage," said Ian.

"Thank you for coming," said Ab, "see you again in Zion. Goodbye for now." And to the sound of applause from every single person in the carriage Ian departed, still with nothing to eat, but so pleased he had opened the door between the carriages.

The only other recent visitors to this carriage had been Ian's cousin Dafydd, and Nick O'Demus who had joined the train at Abergavenny. Amazingly Ab had not mentioned their visit to Ian so he did not realize they had been there. But it would not be long before he would see them again.

Chapter 19

The Ticket Inspector

James, Trevor, Matthieu, and the Professor were still at lunch. Ian's new friend was asleep in his seat. So Ian sat in the vacant seat next to the tramp and tried to forget that he was hungry. It was quiet on the train, very quiet. Everybody was keeping themselves to themselves behind broadsheets, or covering their ears with headphones so they could only hear the music they chose for themselves, or looking at their smartphones to see their own personal selection of fake news, cats doing tricks or elephants swimming the channel.

But the peace was broken when the door at the other end of Ian's carriage opened abruptly and a man with a pointy hat, a black uniform, and an officious demure marched in. He prowled around looking for someone vulnerable to speak to. Everyone else gave the impression they had seen this man before and tried to avoid his gaze. This official made a beeline for Ian.

"Can I see your ticket please?" the man said, half expecting Ian not to be able to produce a valid ticket. Ian always kept his ticket close to his heart in a safe place in his jacket. Carefully he took out his precious ticket and showed it to the inspector.

"That is not a valid ticket," the inspector said. "You did not buy that ticket, you did not pay for it with your wages, you did not earn it; it looks like one of those tickets that were given out free by mistake by the Controller's son a few months ago." All this sounded as if it could be true, so Ian started to doubt that he did have a valid ticket after all. "What do I need to do?" asked Ian foolishly. He had still not had his lunch and he could well have got angry with the inspector. The inspector replied, "You need to be a

94

good Christian, attend church every Sunday, give to charity, be nice to your neighbors, keep the ten commandments, and sign here for a re-education course on ticket purchase. Once you have done all this, then, and only then, do you have a right to buy a ticket, and you must buy replacement tickets from me. Please surrender your ticket to me now."

Ian recalled that some of his friends back in South Wales had done all these things that the inspector had required, and had been issued with a ticket that was not unlike Ian's ticket but without the magnetic strip that opened the gate. They were also a slightly different color, not the true blood red color of Ian's ticket. Some of these friends had tried to use their tickets (which had cost them nearly a year's wages) to make a journey, but the tickets didn't work; they didn't open the narrow gate to the platform for the train to Zion. (This gate could be recognized by the advertisement for a beautiful pearl necklace next to it). The ticket seemed to work on the wider gates to the other platforms that led to the trains destined for lots of other places, but not the train that led to Zion.

Ian plucked up courage to argue. He told the inspector that though he had tried to do all these things, he had failed, but was given a free ticket by the Controller's son, which had already been validated as authentic as it had opened the gate on the platform to this train. Suddenly feeling empowered, Ian went on to say: "Flee from me inspector, my ticket is genuine, you are a deceiver, a wolf in sheep's clothing. You have no right to inspect my ticket. You rebelled against the ticket inspectors' union that the Controller set up; you left to form your own union. Your union is not recognized by the Company as fit to judge who can be on the train to Zion. In fact, I am a bit surprised the Controller let you on this train at all. Be gone!"

With that the inspector was gone seeking someone else to devour.

"Well done," said a voice behind him. It was Dafydd. He and Nick had returned from the next carriage.

"I am so pleased that inspector is gone. While you were away, he was causing all sorts of upset in this carriage. People were starting to shout at each other, to promise to do all the things the inspector demanded. Some nearly signed his form, and others nearly surrendered their tickets. The only one to stand up to him was this tramp that had been asleep in your seat. That is why everyone was so quiet when the inspector returned to inspect your ticket. Well done indeed; you told him where to go," said Nick, so proud of his friend Ian.

Just then Matthieu also returned. He had with him the most wonderful sandwich prepared just for Ian, and delivered by Matthieu at just the right time, for Ian was ravenous by then.

Then the train seemed to slow down, it appeared to be going uphill and round a bend away from the direct route to Zion.

Chapter 20

Death Valley

THE NEXT STOP ON the journey was Death Valley. Ian had desperately want-ed to find out how the tramp had resisted the ticket inspector, to tell them all about Ab and Faith, and show them his presents, but the announcement of the next stop put an end to all that.

It was a dark shadowy place that few relished traveling through, yet it was a place where, it was said, you could meet the Controller himself. According to the Terms and Conditions of Travel on the train to Zion, the Controller had promised to provide safe passage for all staff in the company who needed to travel through this valley. He had also promised to make it a comfortable part of the journey, despite the reputation of the place. It was said to be a fearful place, strewn with corpses of those who had died of thirst. It was a place full of enemies too, who halted trains that tried to pass through the valley, then cut off the supply of food and water, so that the passengers slowly died of thirst and starvation. Then the vultures would come and turn the valley of thirsty passengers into a valley of dry bones.

Yet the Controller had promised to provide abundant water and food there in Death Valley right in front of these enemies. To do this he had established two hotels in this wilderness. They were part of a worldwide chain of his; they were called *Goodness* and *Mercy*.

So, as the train to Zion approached this particular station, Ian had mixed feelings, fear and excitement at the same time.

Then suddenly, just as Ian glimpsed the station sign, he fell violently sick. He could not even get up to go to the toilet he was so ill. He saw a great boil appear on his face. Someone called for a doctor immediately. Without delay, the Controller's own personal doctor responded to the call and was seeing to Ian.

"You have cancer, Ian, you are going to die, set your house in order," the good doctor said, and walked back down the corridor of the train.

Ian turned away, faced the window so that nobody could see his face, and he prayed silently: "Surely, Lord, I have been a good person (one of the best since David they used to say). I have sincerely sought to do all that I felt you wanted me to do. I got on the right train didn't I? I have a valid ticket for this train. I have read the Terms and Conditions of Travel; I know what the Controller has said about this place. I have not yet seen all this land though, not met all the people on this train, and hardly met any people from the other trains; I am too young to die. I have not made use of my gifts yet either; I have done nothing with my plumbing skills since I was an apprentice. There are so many good people back in Wales that I need to tell about my journey, surely this can't be my end here like this?"

Ian wept.

The Controller's doctor was making his way back to his seat when he got another message from the Controller: "Go back to Ian, tell him he will get well again in three days time."

Now, for the doctor, this presented quite a dilemma. He had just told Ian that he was going to die, how could he now go back and tell him he was not going to die. He would look silly. After struggling with these thoughts, the doctor felt he should do what the Controller had told him to do, after all he was the Controller and he had always been right before. So he swallowed his pride, turned round, and made his way through what was now quite an anxious crowd to deliver the Controller's second message to Ian.

The doctor also put an ointment made of mud, spittle, and dried figs on Ian's cancerous boil.

The next day, Ian was still alive and feeling a little better. He called for the doctor and asked him to provide proof that he really would get better within the three days. Ian had never been healed of anything before, let alone cancer. He remembered how Dafydd had said he had been healed of his blindness, a fact he could hardly deny, but now it was personal to him—a matter of life and death. He needed to be sure. He had also been confused by the contradictory diagnoses, from the same doctor given within minutes of each other. What had happened to change the doctor's mind he wondered? Could it be that his prayers had been answered? Could it be that he had more to do before he reached the end of his journey or was this the end for Ian?

Ian had been an apprentice plumber back in Talybont and he had had a desire when he was younger to do something to help provide water in Africa to those who had to get water from rivers or wells miles away, but he had never done anything about this calling. Perhaps he could now do something for the travelers through Death Valley. So to be absolutely sure that his cancer was going to disappear and never return, he asked the Controller's doctor for a strange proof.

The doctor felt the Controller owed him something for making him look stupid by giving him these two seemingly contradictory messages. The doctor had faith in the Controller to provide the necessary proof that Ian had asked for. In fact the doctor felt that the Controller should provide something really dramatic to make up for the embarrassment of the last twenty-four hours. Someone being healed of cancer in three days was completely unknown in the doctor's experience. He felt dramatic proof that this was to happen should be provided. He offered Ian a choice of two extraordinary proofs, without even checking with the Controller if these were possible. He said, "Would you like the train to go back ten stations or go forward ten stations?"

Ian replied that he would like to see the train go back ten stations, as it was easy for the train to go forward ten stations. The doctor was the representative of the Controller on the train for all matters of health. The Controller's reputation was at stake, so even though the doctor had not consulted him earlier, the Controller agreed to the request that the train go back ten stations. And so it did. Nobody knew how it happened but everybody on the train saw it happen.

After this Ian determined to make the most of the remaining time he had been granted, fifteen years in fact. He had great faith that he would be able to do something lasting, something worthwhile, something special with the rest of his life. He set about designing, and then constructing a conduit with the help of his four remaining traveling companions: his cousin Dafydd, Nick O'Demus, Matthieu, and the tramp who had fallen asleep in Ian's seat. They collected all the equipment they needed from the ten additional stops the train made. Then they built a new system to bring water onto the train so that everybody could drink their fill of fresh water while they were on the train, even when travelling through Death Valley. This invention, known as "Ian's Conduit," worked very well and is still in use today. An example can be seen in *The Museum of the Train* at York, and the original is in the city of Zion itself, for all to see.

Chapter 21

What Do You See?

IAN, AS RIGHT AS rain now, was enjoying the view from his seat having left Death Valley behind them. Five fellow travelers who were sitting near to him in his carriage were also looking out of the window. Suddenly, out of the blue, as they turned a corner, the sun shone directly into their window. They were almost blinded by the intensity of the light. Each of them reached for their sunglasses to cut down the light that they could not stand. Each one had a different type of sunglasses.

"What do you see out of the window? Do those glasses help you see more clearly?" Ian asked the man opposite him.

He was a professor of physics, and his glasses were very impressive; the frames were made of titanium, and the lenses were highly polarized, so that half of the light from the sun was completely absorbed. The photons that did manage to make it to his eyes were very carefully examined by his highly tuned academic brain.

He commenced; "I see light from our nearest star that we call the sun. I see the result of a nuclear explosion thousands of years ago that happened at the center of our star. I see hydrogen changing into helium; I see electron pairs orbiting neutrons and protons, which are bound together by gluons. Deeper still I see up and down quarks, and I glimpse their brothers—charm, strange, top, and bottom;—their cousins the leptons—electron, muon, tau, and their neutrino partners,—and I see the bosons—gluon, Z, W—. . . oh, and a new member of their family—Higgs, we have been searching for him for years, decades in fact, and we have at last found him, and we have just welcomed him into the family with a big party. However, above all, I see a photon, that massless chargeless boson that carries the electromagnetic force, which enables electric lights, motors, washing machines, lasers, and all of electronics to work.

"Light has color," continued the professor, "as you can see in a rainbow, but if you look very carefully you will see some missing colors. I can see from these missing colors what the universe is made of. Some of these missing colors are redder than they should be and from this I can see that the universe is expanding and that it appears to be about 13 billion years old. But its rate of expansion seems to be increasing. This is one of many puzzling things that I see that I do not yet understand:

- Why is the rate of expansion of the universe increasing?
- Could this expansion be explained by dark matter hidden somewhere in the universe?
- Why hasn't the whole universe turned to iron?
- Why is the universe so ordered when it should become increasingly disordered?
- How do particles that are quantum pairs communicate with each other over billions of miles?
- Why are we made of matter rather than anti-matter?
- What was there before the big bang?
- What will happen to the universe eventually?"

"I see," said Ian, not entirely convinced that he did see.

Looking for some lighter conversation, he turned to a lady wearing a pink, black and yellow dress which seemed to be advertising daffodils from the Scilly Isles. She had put on a pair of rose-tinted sunglasses which nestled in her red hair that looked like it had been dragged through a hedge backwards.

"And what do you see?" Ian asked her.

"I see daffodils," she replied.

> "I wandered lonely as a cloud
> That floats on high o'er vales and hills,
> When all at once I saw a crowd,
> A host, of golden daffodils;
> Beside the lake, beneath the trees,
> Fluttering and dancing in the breeze.

Continuous as the stars that shine
And twinkle on the Milky Way,
They stretched in never-ending line
Along the margin of a bay:
Ten thousand saw I at a glance,
Tossing their heads in sprightly dance.

The waves beside them danced; but they
Out-did the sparkling waves in glee:
A poet could not but be gay,
In such a jocund company:
I gazed—and gazed—but little thought
What wealth the show to me had brought:

For oft, when on my couch I lie
In vacant or in pensive mood,
They flash upon that inward eye
Which is the bliss of solitude;
And then my heart with pleasure fills,
And dances with the daffodils.[17]

"That is how I see life, my young friend. Would you like to hear one of my own compositions, it is called the 'Pink Daisy'?"

By now Ian had worked out that she was a poet, and did she know it! Ian was just trying to compose a polite way of declining this offer when he was saved by his third companion, Professor Demas, who interrupted brusquely, "I just saw a near miss!" he shouted. "Didn't you see it?" he exclaimed incredulously as none of the other occupants of the carriage seemed to have seen it.

"Where?" Ian asked tentatively.

"Just back there at the level crossing." Well only one of the other passengers had even seen the level crossing let alone the "near miss". The man who had seen the "near miss" was a man in his fifties or sixties. He wore a worn tweed jacket repaired lovingly with brown leather patches on the elbows. His glasses were of a classical style, the plastic frames were brown/beige/sand colored, and the lenses were dark and very dusty. He too was an academic, from the same university as our physicist but they had never met, never spoken in fact. He was from the history department and his special interest was level crossings.

"I saw a man wearing earphones, on a bike, dart round the closed gates having just avoided colliding with our train!" he recounted excitedly.

"I have a sharp eye for tragic events," he said. "I have researched the history of level crossing accidents since 1816. Would you like to hear my lecture on my research on the causes of pedestrian accidents at level crossings? . . . I can give you just the summary if you like."

Our history lecturer had noticed a slight reluctance on the part of the five new students in his captive audience, so, rather than offer the full lecture, he proceeded only with the summary, surmising that once they had been enlightened by the summary they would surely want to hear the full lecture. This was his abbreviated summary:

"The aims of the research were to establish the underlying causes of pedestrian accidents at level crossings, understand the reasons why they occur, and examine solutions both existing and novel. The research reached the following general conclusions about pedestrian risk at level crossings:

- Overall, the number of pedestrian accidents is strongly linked to the number of pedestrians, and the number of trains.

- Accidents are more common at station crossings, with male users, and increase with age above thirty.

- At specific locations, combinations of characteristics of users, trains, the crossing layout, and equipment may 'add up' to cause users to have particular difficulties in crossing safely. This supports the idea that improved site-specific hazard assessments should be carried out alongside the quantitative risk assessment.

- The research suggests marking a colored 'danger zone' to highlight the area in which users are at risk from being struck by a train."[18]

"Thank you for your fascinating insight into the world of level crossings," Ian interjected before he could proceed to the full lecture.

Ian mused that through the same window over the same few minutes his three fellow travelers had seen three completely different things; one had seen the universe expanding, another a field of daffodils, and the third a level crossing near miss. Was it the glasses they had chosen to wear that had filtered the information coming through the window in a different way? Was it their education that had taught them what information to focus on and what to ignore? Was it their culture, their personality, their motivation or just chance?

Next was a young lad wearing some very fancy sunglasses, they seemed like mirrors reflecting the scenes passing by so others could see what was rushing past but not the young lad himself. He had gone for double Polaroids. One layer absorbed all the light of one polarization, and the second layer (oriented perpendicular) absorbed all the rest of the light, consequently our young lad saw next to nothing. He was quite happy with this view though; he could listen to his music, he did not really care to see his follow passengers, and he was not at all interested in what was going on outside the train. And he thought his shades looked rather cool, so he wore them all the time.

"What did you see?" Ian asked him, after digging him in the shoulder to get his attention.

"Nothing," the young lad replied.

Actually he had seen a few shapes, some bright moments, and some dark moments, but he wasn't going to let on, and none of the other passengers wanted to show any further interest in him so that was that.

Our fifth fellow traveler in the carriage was also an academic. He was from the same department as our level crossing historian. He was dressed all in black, with a blood red tie and a pin which resembled a serpent. His glasses were dark too, but they looked as if they had been in the wars. They were all scratched and blood-stained, so it was hard for him to see through them. However, he was able to perceive a crimson picture of the scene from the window.

"And what do you see?" Ian asked the man with the blood-stained glasses, slightly worried about what he would hear.

"I saw a blood bath," the man replied. "I saw a fight between two men; one black and one white. I saw a car accident. I saw a mother lash out at her two-year-old son. I saw a generation of suffering on the face of a man just out of prison. I saw a plague across the face of the earth. I saw the vain attempts of a policeman to talk sense into a crowd of revelers bent on enjoying themselves, and not caring about passing the deadly plague onto their grandparents. I saw a man in a crusader outfit going to a stag party, and in this I saw the centuries of Christian and Muslim persecution of the Jews as well as a callous ignorance of history in today's way of celebrating the marriage of two people."

"Didn't you see the wild donkeys running freely, the ostriches flapping their wings with joy, and the powerful hippopotamus eating his lunch under the lotus plant? Didn't you see the children sitting in the marketplace calling one to another, and playing music for you even though you would not dance?" Ian replied, rather surprised at his own poetic tone.

Ian continued his questioning of the man with the blood-stained glasses, "Didn't you see the warning signs about violence leading to violence, and why plagues come to the earth? Didn't you see the 'ten words' from the Controller on the billboard? Couldn't you see the lessons from the history of the Middle East, when a vast people were exiled to Babylon when they refused to heed the ten words or respond to the many diverse calls from the Controller for them to return to him? Couldn't you read the writing on the wall?

"Didn't you see the love shown by the Controller's son when he gave up his life to save others? Didn't you see the signs recorded by John Four; the water turned into wine, the deaf hearing, the dumb speaking, and the lame walking? Didn't you see how the Controller's son wept when his friend died, and how he made him alive again? Didn't you see the eyewitness account of 550 people saying they had seen the Controller's son alive again after he had been killed? Didn't you see how his twelve followers were transformed from fishermen and tax-collectors to leaders of a new company, willing to die for their beliefs?"

Ian realized that he wasn't wearing sunglasses anymore; he must have taken them off. He could see through the window clearly now, he could see everything as it really was. His eyes had adjusted to the brightness of the sun; he had no need to avert his eyes from the brightness of the view from the window. He could now see the sunlight as photons from the nuclear reaction at the center of a star, but also as golden daffodils beside the lake beneath the trees, as enlightenment from careful research designed to save lives from train accidents. Even in the shadowy dark world of nothingness he could see. Even in the violence, wars and plagues he could see some light (though only dimly), and certainly he could see the work and provision of the Controller, and all that his son had achieved that meant that this very train was now able to make its way along this track towards Zion with such a motley crew on board.

The next night Ian could not sleep. He couldn't help thinking about the five passengers with the five different glasses, all seeing the world so differently. Why, Ian was pondering, do people see the world so differently? Was it the glasses they see through or was it that they chose the glasses to wear to suit how they want to see the world? Why does one choose jet-black glasses and another rose-tinted glasses?

Ian had his thinking glasses on now, when it was really time to put on his sleeping glasses, but he could not help himself. Who manufactures the glasses? Who designs them? Do they do it for profit or to help people to see better? What influences the choice of glasses? Is it our parents who buy our first pair, is it peer pressure, our wish to look like our friends and see things the same way they do? Or is it the companies who advertise the glasses who are the ones who really determine which glasses we wear? Maybe it is our education, or perhaps our beliefs, our personality, our intelligence, or our political party?

It was dark outside now, the time to sleep, but inside for Ian it was bright, a time to think, not a time to sleep. The light wasn't pure white, it did not contain all the colors of the spectrum so his thinking was not completely objective. It was colored by his environment, the faint yellowish light in the train, and how it reflected off the brown seats and the brown wooden coachwork. It was in this light that he pondered, ever more deeply.

We elect politicians, so we choose who we think are best to govern our lands. Perhaps they choose our glasses, or if they don't, perhaps they should, or at least surely they influence how we see the world to some degree, after all they determine how we are educated. Or perhaps it is all down to our DNA, though then twins would always choose the same glasses, and they don't.

Do people realize others are wearing very different glasses? Is this how disputes arise, how wars start? Some people force others in their group to wear the same type of glasses (at least in public), other groups don't care what you wear but then wonder why their members disagree on almost everything.

Is it possible to travel through life without a pair of glasses at all?

This was Ian's final question before his musing was brought to an abrupt halt by a young man dressed in a white coat coming through the train. "Can I have your glasses please," he said.

The man in the white coat was pulling a small trolley, on which were some black boxes with some strange symbols on the side: →★.

"Two blasts with this laser and you will have perfect vision," he said. "You will be able to throw away your glasses and see the world how it really is."

He hadn't had many customers that night. Most preferred the darkness, to hide from the realities of life, and from the consequences of their own deeds or maybe the middle of the night wasn't the best time to consider eye surgery. So only a few had agreed to the treatment, but these few were now freed from seeing life from a single narrow angle, and could now see clearly, understand the point of view of others, see all the needs around them as well as the amazing variety of the beauty of the world and its inhabitants.

Following behind the man in the white coat came a wispy old lady carrying a pair of golden tweezers. "Let me remove the specks in your eyes, clear away the dust, the splinters, and the logs that have accumulated to stop you seeing clearly," she offered. Sadly she did not have many customers either. Most people did not even see her because their sight was so poor. They did not realize all the rubbish that had accumulated in their eyes over the years and so they missed the opportunity to see clearly again. But this did not stop those with the most cluttered eyes seeing the tiny specks in other people's eyes. Ian thought that was strange.

Despite the darkness around him, and most other people ignoring these offers, Ian agreed to the laser surgery, and to the golden tweezers. And yes he could see, could he see indeed!! It was as if someone had turned up the brightness tenfold on the computer screen, now he could distinguish so many more colors. He could even discern the lines in the spectrum that identified different types of light source. How happy Ian was to have agreed to this, and how sad he was that so few of his fellow travelers had even been prepared to consider it.

Chapter 22

Cleaning Windows

AFTER THE EXTRAORDINARILY DIFFERENT views seen through the train window by the passengers wearing different glasses, Ian took a greater interest in the view from the train window. He wondered if his view could be improved further if the windows were properly cleaned. So, with his own handkerchief, he cleaned part of the window next to him. He peered through the section he had cleaned and compared it with the rest of the window; the difference was remarkable. Ian had not realized how dirty the windows had become. He then went into the next carriage and did the same thing there. This let a shaft of light into the carriage, rather like in an old master's painting where the sun peeks through a hole in the clouds to illuminate the subject. Ian found it was the same with all the windows in the train. So he called the cleaning supervisor and asked why all the windows were so dirty.

"Oh you have noticed, have you?" the supervisor said.

"Yes," said Ian. "And I would like to know why they are so dirty."

"OK, I will tell you," replied the supervisor, looking pleased that at last someone had noticed the dirty windows, and happy to recount the tale that explained the state of the windows.

"Many centuries ago, one morning the Controller's son hired some window cleaners. He agreed a wage of £100 for the day. They were pleased with this, as it was more than they got on other jobs cleaning windows. So, with a cheery tune, off they went cleaning the windows, enjoying the summer sunshine, and so happy to bring new light into the train.

"At the next stop two more window cleaners were standing idle on the platform. 'Go onto the train and clean the windows,' said the Controller's son, 'and I will pay you a fair wage.' So without signing a contract or anything they got on and started work quite contentedly. At the next two stops exactly the same thing happened, and so four more workers were taken on with the same words. Finally, at the penultimate stop of the day, the Controller's son saw four young lads kicking a ball around on the platform. They had carefully placed their buckets upside down towards the end of the platform to form two goals. 'What are you doing?' he called out to them. 'Nobody has given us any work today so we are playing soccer' they replied.

"'I will give you a job' the Controller's son said. 'Jump on and I will pay you whatever is right.'

"They were by now fed up with their game, so were pleased to get a job for the last hour of the day; hopefully they might get enough for a beer they thought.

"When the train arrived at the terminal station that night the Controller's son called the window cleaners to his office and got out the wage packets for them. He paid those who had been playing soccer for most of the day £100, even though they had done less than an hour's work. They were so pleased, what amazing generosity, we don't deserve that much they thought. They were happy to pocket their wages and didn't argue about it!

"The rest of the window cleaners were then given their wages. Those who had been hired at the first stop, and had worked all day, had now assumed that they would get at least £800, as they had done eight times as much work. However, when they opened their wage packets they were very disappointed, only £100. They grumbled to the Controller's son. 'These guys worked less than an hour and they got the same as us,' they moaned. 'But we agreed £100,' reasoned the Controller's son. 'You seemed very happy with that this morning. Don't I have the right to be generous to the unemployed if I want to? I have done you no wrong, be content with what you have and go your way.'

"So off they went, but they were not content. That evening they called a meeting of the Rail Section of the window cleaners' union and told everybody there how unfair the Controller's son had been to them. 'Victimization,' they shouted. 'All out!' So before the meeting had had a chance to properly consider what the Controller's son had done, a strike motion had been passed and an official strike was declared for the next day. None of the window cleaners were prepared to cross the picket line. They all chose to avoid work on trains from that day forth, despite other work paying well under £100 a day. Even the young lads who had received £100 for their hour's work didn't cross the picket line, they were afraid of the pickets, so they too went off to do other work.

"And that, my friend, is why the windows on trains are always dirty."

Chapter 23

Three Wise Men

IAN THEN LEFT THE cleaning supervisor and walked up the train to a new carriage. He took his seat next to three men, Mr Parry Jones, a rail engineer, Professor Heisenberg, the physicist he had met earlier, and Mr Lambert—a theologian. Ian felt as if he was sitting next to three very wise men. The gifts they were carrying were not gold, frankincense, and myrrh, but insight, understanding, and knowledge.

Ian opened up the conversation by talking about the weather; after all he was from Wales.

"It is strange how the forecast turns out to be wrong so often isn't it?" Ian commenced.

"How true," replied the rail engineer.

"Actually that is true of a lot of things. We think we have understood something but when we look more carefully, we find we are often mistaken. That is true in my field of rail engineering and I would guess it is true in your fields too?" he said looking at the other two 'wise men'.

"Would you be interested to hear an example or two of insights that have altered over the last century or so in train travel?" offered the rail engineer.

The other two wise men were open minded and always interested to hear insights from other worldviews, so they said yes. Ian was happy to listen in on their conversation too.

"I have been researching how insights have changed over time and I have produced a paper on the subject. Here is the summary table from my paper." The rail engineer delved into his rather scruffy black ruck-sack he had been given at the Rail Industry Association's first Innovation conference and dug out three copies of this table which he presented to Ian, and to the other two wise men.

Table of Insights (Rail)

What we thought we knew	What we now think we know
1. Seat belts improve safety	1. Seat belts on trains reduce safety because it takes longer to evacuate
2. Smoking on trains is acceptable	2. Smoking on trains is unacceptable because it causes cancer even to passive smokers
3. Travel by train is less reliable than by car	3. In fact the mean delay by train is 5 minutes (when traveling 200km) by road it is 20 minutes
4. Trees next to rail lines are good, as they reduce noise and improve the view	4. Leaves on the line cause delays, as there is a risk of skidding
5. Trees next to rail lines are bad because the leaves on the line can cause trains to skid leading to delays	5. Cutting down trees next to rail lines can be risky as shading is reduced and in summer tracks may buckle
6. Signals on sticks are safer than people waving red or green flags	6. LED lights are better than signals as they are brighter and cheaper
7. Signaling equipment within the train cab is cheaper and more efficient than line side signals	7. Central control of trains is better as capacity can be increased and driver error reduced
8. Train windows should be shut, so the air conditioning can work efficiently	8. Train windows should be open to stop any virus recirculating

The rail engineer turned to the physicist and asked, "Has there been anything new in the world of physics that could compare with the advances in rail engineering?"

"Has there been? I should say so!" replied the physicist rather indignantly; he had thought the rail engineer would have at least grasped the basics of advances in quantum mechanics that had happened since 1905.

So he produced a table from a book he had written a few years ago. It was remarkably similar to the rail engineer's:

Table of Insights (Physics)

What we thought we knew	What we now think we know
1. The earth is flat	1. The earth is spherical
2. The sun goes round the earth	2. The earth goes round the sun
3. The earth goes round the sun.	3. All motion is relative, the earth travels in a straight line in the curved space-time around the sun
4. Matter is solid	4. Matter is mainly empty space with an occasional atom
5. Atoms are solid and indivisible	5. Atoms are made of protons, neutrons, electrons and empty space
6. Protons, neutrons, and electrons are solid and indivisible fundamental particles	6. Protons are made of quarks (two ups and a down), and a bunch of gluons
7. Time advances at the same rate everywhere	7. Time slows down near dense objects like black holes or neutron stars
8. Knowing the speed and position of something you can work out exactly where it will be in the future	8. You can never know the speed & position of anything exactly; uncertainty of position x uncertainty of (speed x mass) $>5\text{x}10^{-35}$ J.sec

"People think physics and engineering are exact sciences, and what is 'proved' is certain," said Ian. The theologian nodded in agreement.

"That is what people think but it is not the case. As we look more closely at the world we live in, the more we realize that what we thought we knew is not so. Science only provides theories that seem to match our observations, nothing more; so as we get better at making observations we have to change what we believe about the world," replied the physicist.

"What about your field?" the physicist asked the theologian, who had been listening quietly up to this point.

"Well, yes," the theologian replied. "There are many perceptions that people have that are wrong in my field too, as demonstrated by experience. But there is one difference, we have a book inspired by the one who claims to have created the universe, and sent his son to tell us about it. So my advice is to read the book and test what it says by putting into practice what you can. That way just like in physics you will see if the theory proposed in the book is a good explanation of what we experience in life. And just as physics enables some degree of predicting what will happen in the future, so this book predicts what will happen to you in the future, including after you die, so I think you should at least read it, and test what it says before you die, then you will have more confidence about what will happen to you in the end."

"Sounds logical," said the physicist.

"Let me show you my table," continued the theologian. On the left you see some traditional views, what many people thought they knew. On the right you see what the book says, some of which you can test by experiment before you die, particularly items 5 to 8:

Table of Insights (Spiritual Wisdom)

What we thought we knew (traditional wisdom)	What we now know (from the book)
1. Good deeds will get you to heaven (probably)	1. By grace you are saved through faith in the Son of God
2. All roads lead to God	2. "I am the way, and the truth, and the life; no one comes to the Father but through Me."[19] Jesus Christ
3. Surely hell doesn't exist	3. "Fear Him who is able to destroy both soul and body in hell"[20] Jesus Christ
4. If I attend church twice a year I should be OK	4. The church is the body of believers, not a building. There were no church buildings when the book was written
5. Give to Christian charities and you will have less money	5. "Give, and it will be given to you."[21] "He who sows bountifully will also reap bountifully."[22]

Table of Insights (Spiritual Wisdom)

6. I have the right to get my own back on those who attack me	6. "Vengeance is Mine"[23] says God. "whoever slaps you on your right cheek, turn the other to him also"[24] Jesus Christ
7. God did not have a son. The fastest way to heaven is martyrdom	7. "For God so loved the world, that He gave His only begotten Son, that whoever believes in Him shall not perish, but have eternal life"[25]
8. Miracles don't really happen	8. "'Go; your faith has made you well.' Immediately he regained his sight and began following Him"[26]

"So," the theologian concluded, "I say we should not be arrogant but rather humble, testing things against the book and then see what actually happens. Traditional spiritual wisdom can be wrong, just as traditional theories of matter, gravity, and time can be wrong. People's perceptions can often be misplaced, like thinking that train travel is less reliable than travel by car, where careful measurements of what actually happens point to the opposite conclusion. So what past generations have handed down to us may not always be very helpful. I would challenge you to look for yourself at the evidence, test for yourself the claims of the book, and then you can be at peace as you lie on your death-bed having honestly sought the truth."

"Thank you" said the quantum mechanics professor "I will read your book and test what it says for myself."

"I will do the same" promised the engineer.

"What about you?" Ian was asked.

"I have already read most of it and found it so true to life. I promise to read the rest of it and let you know how I get on putting it into practice" replied Ian as he searched in his bag for his copy to show his new fellow travellers.

Chapter 24

The Shiloh Rail Line

IAN WAS HAPPY HE had spent time sitting with the quantum mechanics professor, the rail engineer, and the theologian, but now he spotted three other people in the carriage he had not noticed before and felt drawn to sit with them. They were a civil engineer, a mechanical engineer, and another rail historian.

"May I?" Ian asked politely as he took his seat next to them.

"Be my guest," said the civil engineer.

"Look out of the window, there is the Shiloh rail line!" announced the rail historian excitedly.

"Looked like a Class 77B to me," said the mechanical engineer.

"Lovely little station; two island platforms just like the first station ever built," said the civil engineer, who hadn't noticed the steam engine pass by.

"Now lads don't argue about what you saw," said the rail historian. "I am sure Ian here would like to hear the history of how the Shiloh rail line was built; it is quite an instructive lesson for us who are interested in rail systems."

Both the engineers were over sixty, so hardly lads, and they were bent on continuing their argument about the most important features of the Shiloh rail line, but happily Ian replied to the historian that he would indeed like to hear the tale of the Shiloh rail line, so, before either of the engineers could say another word, our historian started his history lesson.

"Way back when they were constructing the original rail line to Zion a group of civil engineers had just completed phase I of the project and the

Controller had sent them off to the far side of the river to plan the route for phase II.

"All the land to build the rail line had been acquired, planning permission had been obtained, funds raised, and all the staff trained. Though there had been some battles over phase I, the company had been successful, and had overcome all the obstacles. The civil works were just about done. The mechanical engineers, and the signaling engineers, still had plenty of work to do on phase I, so there was a separation between the civils and the rest of the work force. Therefore 77 percent of the company employees stayed where they were, but 23 percent were relocated beyond the river, which suited them because that is where their families lived.

"Several months later a picture appeared in the Rail Gazette of a new rail line with the caption; 'Civils build rival rail line beyond the river'. The 77 percent who had remained to finish off phase I were incensed. How dare the civils build a rival rail system, complete with signals, engines, and carriages! How on earth had they managed to do this in such a short time, and without *our* help! They have broken the union agreement on demarcation; they have dishonored the company, and the Controller too. The rumor spread quickly among the staff working on phase I. Nobody bothered to check the facts. The source of the picture in the paper was not given, there was not even any accompanying text, but the gossip spread and dissension grew.

"Prior to this, the staff were a friendly united workforce, now they were separating into two factions. Everybody was willing to listen to this gossip; they paid more attention to this than to their own work.

"It was just a photo, but they had assumed that it meant that this group of civil engineers had secretly set up a rival rail company to build a separate rail line to Zion, deliberately concealing it from them.

"The mechanical engineers in particular were up in arms. They called an emergency general meeting of the Institution of Mechanical Engineers. It was war now with their brother and sister engineers across the river. The fact that both groups were members of the Trade Union Congress counted for nothing.

"Ten senior delegates were elected to form an action committee to confront the rebel civil engineers. An e-mail to them was drafted, consulted on, and sent off in less than a week—a speed of response rarely seen before within the institution. This is what it said:

This memorandum has been agreed by the whole membership of the Institution of Mechanical Engineers.

What is this disloyal act that you have committed against the express instructions of the Controller, deviating from the agreed plan for the construction of a single rail line to Zion? We have seen a photograph of the rail line you have constructed at Shiloh and we consider it to be an act of rebellion against the company as well as a betrayal of us your brothers and sisters in the Trades Union Congress. Was not the disaster of the establishment of separate institutions of civil and mechanical rail engineering enough? Now you are even building complete rail systems yourself.

However, we would like to make an offer of reconciliation to you. Return to us on this side of the river, re-integrate with us, and we will provide land and houses for you and your families, only do not rebel against the Controller by building this rival rail line. Remember how the whole company suffered, including many engineers, the last time something like this happened.

For and on behalf of the Institution of Mechanical Engineers,

Professor Sir Fin Ahaz

Earl of Glossop, President of the Institution of Mechanical Engineers
cc The Rail Controller

"When this e-mail arrived in the office of the Institution of Civil Engineers across the river they could hardly believe it. Was it April 1st? Had the I. Mech. E. e-mail account been hacked? No, after doing all the necessary checks they concluded that the e-mail was genuine. So the President of the Institution of Civil Engineers, General Joshua Eisenhower, immediately formed a sub-committee of senior managers, and headed off to Shiloh to investigate.

"And this is what they discovered. A couple of old retired civil engineers, Fred Reuben, and Arthur Gad, had conceived the idea of building a model rail line at Shiloh, where Phase I of the line to Zion ends, and where Phase II starts, just by the river. They thought it would be a good reminder of the line to Zion. It would remind future generations of the origins of the rail line, and the unique way to Zion. They used their life savings to pay for it. They worked night and day to get it finished in record time. They did it to honor the Controller, and the company as a fitting memorial to rail engineering.

"When they had finished it they had taken a photo of it and tried to send it to the Rail Gazette together with an article describing their efforts, but the file size was too large and their e-mail bounced. Helpfully a man from 'Staff Assistance' was able to reduce the resolution of the picture and send it off for them but it got sent without the article, and the cover e-mail only mentioned the headline that a new rail line to Zion had been completed.

"Then the penny dropped. The investigative sub-committee realized what had happened. Because of the poor resolution in the photo, and the omission of the article explaining what had happened, the mechanical engineers on the other side of the river had concluded that the civils had constructed a full-size working rail system, an exact copy, and rival, to the original rail line to Zion specified by the Controller, whereas all they had done was make a nice little model rail line!

"Before any more damage could be done the President of the Civils wisely asked to meet with the President of the Mechanicals; an e-mail reply was not appropriate under the circumstances.

"So the two presidents, and their sub-committees, met at Shiloh the next week. The mechanicals were somewhat red faced when they saw the model. Then a great sense of relief, almost joy, came over them as they realized that their civil brothers and sisters were not setting up a rival rail system after all, they had not dishonored the Controller, and their intentions had been entirely honorable.

"The same day they e-mailed all the members of the Institution of Mechanical Engineers clarifying the position and thanking the Controller for his understanding in forgiving them their misunderstanding.

"They also agreed a corrective action to try to make sure such a misunderstanding never happened again. So they agreed to hold a joint annual conference of rail engineering to facilitate communication, interoperability, and understanding within the wider rail system.

"The first such congress was held at Shiloh, and involved the best dinner ever at the café of the Shiloh model rail line," concluded the rail historian.

Ian had been observing the faces of the civil engineer and the mechanical engineer throughout this account. There had been much huffing and puffing, red faces, and chiding of each other during the telling of this tale. However, as the train to Zion pulled into Shiloh station the two of them alighted together, happy to have each other's company on their visit to the Shiloh model rail line.

A Ticket to Zion

The train to Zion paused its journey to Zion there for any passengers who wished to make a visit to the model rail line.

The rail historian accompanied Ian on the model rail visit. Just in case Ian had not already learnt the lessons of the model rail line at Shiloh, he gave Ian this note which explained the lessons that all travelers to Zion are urged to learn from this incident. This is what the note said:

1. *Check your facts before complaining.*

2. *Don't spread false accusations.*

3. *Don't gossip.*

4. *Don't speak negatively about your brothers or sisters.*

5. *Ignore unattributed gossip.*

6. *Don't pass on gossip, particularly when negative.*

7. *If you hear negative things about others, don't immediately believe it; check very carefully the source of the information first.*

8. *Avoid wrong conclusions based on poor evidence*

9. *Assume good things about others until you have seen and carefully checked evidence to the contrary.*

10. *Be aware that a deceptive "group-think" can easily develop when a group does not look outside its own members' views.*

11. *Don't separate into cliques, come together regularly to exchange views.*

12. *Try to understand why others are saying what seems to you to be stupid.*

13. *Jaw jaw is better than war war.*

14. *If misunderstandings are not resolved they can lead to division, disunity, and discouragement to those thinking of joining the train to Zion.*

"Thank you," said Ian "I shall cherish your note." And with that Ian dug out his book that the theologian had spoken of previously, and placed the note as a bookmark in chapter twenty-two of the sixth book. (The book was actually a book of books rather than a single book.) Ian then returned to his seat happy to have made the effort to meet the engineers and the historian, and to have learnt some important lessons from the history of the Shiloh rail line.

This part of the journey to Zion had been rather quiet and contemplative, and Ian had enjoyed learning some important truths. However, that was about to change.

Chapter 25

Slough

"The next station stop will be Slough," the announcement echoed through the train. "The train will then stop at Royal Windsor."

This announcement, like many announcements before it, started a conversation in Ian's compartment. Rose started by reciting a poem:

"Come, friendly bombs, and fall on Slough!
It isn't fit for humans now,
There isn't grass to graze a cow.
Swarm over, Death!"[27]

"Sir John Betjeman seemed to think Slough was a place to be endured rather than a place to be enjoyed," remarked Dr Why to Rose. Ian had met Rose earlier in the summer just after they had passed through Death Valley. Rose (Ian's friendly poet) was sitting quietly in the corner scribbling verses of poetry on scraps of paper. She was still wearing her pink, black, and yellow dress as well as her rose-tinted spectacles. At the sound of this announcement though, Dr Why and Rose had become unusually animated.

"Yet the friendly bombs did not fall on Slough, I wonder why?" asked Dr Why.

"Why," continued Dr Why, "does the Controller permit Slough to exist at all, why doesn't he just expand the Royal kingdom of Windsor to include the land of Slough, and close down this horrible station as well as the town around it?"

"I used to live in Slough" piped up General Allenby. "It was indeed a horrible place—I was ill the whole time I lived there; I suppose it was the diesel fumes. I was fine when I moved to Windsor."

The general continued "I was despondent when I lived in Slough. My time there got me thinking about my despondency, my suffering, and the inequality in the world as a whole. Why is it that the Controller doesn't just demolish all the below average places in the world, and rebuild them so that they are all average?"

"Well," replied Rose, "to make everywhere equal he would have to demolish the nice places like Windsor as well, and rebuild them as average places. Then there would be no 'highs' and 'lows' in life, no ups and downs, no poetry in life. Each commune would then be the same, perfectly average, grey, and boring—that would be the ultimate triumph for communism," concluded Rose.

"I think I know why the Controller has not sent the friendly bombs on Slough," said the wise old general who had been listening intently to the conversation between Dr Why and Rose.

"Tell us then," they urged him, intrigued.

So the general began his discourse. "Places like Slough are training grounds. The Controller laid out the rail line to Zion so that it would go through Slough first before it got to Royal Windsor. The slough of despond is situated on the way to the riches of Royal Windsor. He wanted us to persevere through Slough, enduring hardship so that we might be trained by the experience, and produce a harvest of peace. That is why the line to Windsor, and to Zion, runs through Slough, and that is why the Controller resisted attempts to bomb the slough of despond out of existence.

"But with the encouragement of all those faithful travelers who have gone before, we can endure, find our way through Slough to Windsor, and eventually to Zion itself. If we do this we will be given crowns of honor when we get there.

"The Controller even promises special help for those passing though Slough. You may be hated, reproached, and ostracized because you are on your way to Zion, but jump for joy, he says, because your reward will be great when you get to Zion. Some of the residents of Slough will even kill some of those on the train to Zion, thinking they are doing what the Controller would want. For those that suffer that fate, he promised a first class high speed train journey across the Channel, and then a thousand years of bliss reigning with him in his kingdom beyond the Channel, before finally reaching their resting place in Zion."

With this discourse finished, the train came to a stop in Slough Station. It waited a very long time; there appeared to be engine trouble, and failed air conditioning in the carriages. Tempers frayed.

All this time Nick and Dafydd had been in another carriage enjoying the journey, slouching in their comfy seats and reminiscing about the old times. But when the air conditioning failed the temperature was raised. Nick said he was getting fed up with the train and was going to get off. Dafydd pleaded with him to stay but he would not listen. So, hot under the collar, out stormed Nick without even trying to find Ian to say goodbye.

Then just after Nick had gone Dafydd heard what he thought was gunfire, followed by people screaming. Doors opened and out ran many passengers onto the platform to escape. The police arrived, then a fleet of ambulances. There was blood; people were wounded. Dr Why tried to do what he could for a young lady who had collapsed next to the exit on platform two, but it was too late. Five people had been shot, and three of these had lost their lives. It was a terrorist attack by a fanatical group who had been brought up to hate the train to Zion and all the Zionists, as they called them, who were on the train.

One of the passengers who died was the rail historian who had recounted the tale of the Shiloh rail line to Ian. Nick had avoided being shot by running away from the station and from the train to Zion. He vowed never to return. A great sadness fell upon Ian, but at the same time a peculiar strength to persevere. Matthieu and Charles (the tramp) had managed to hide in the toilets during the attack. They were so pleased to be reunited with Ian. As the general predicted, some on the train had left at Slough, and others had lost their lives to the terrorists. It was all over the front pages of the papers the next day. The nation was perplexed; nobody seemed to know why this had happened or what to do.

Then suddenly with a jerk the train was off again, this time mended, tested, and strengthened by its extended stop in Slough, and now gaining speed along the river for the ascent up the hill to Windsor Castle, where all the passengers were treated to a tour of the royal estate by the Controller's son, and given a miniature souvenir crown of jewels. This was, however, but a brief interlude in a testing time for all those on the train to Zion.

Chapter 26

The Test Track

"Welcome to the test track," read the sign as the train to Zion took a sharp turn off the main line down into a deep valley called 'The Shadow of Death.' Dafydd had been that way before, and looked everywhere on the train to find his cousin. Dafydd knew this next part of the journey was going to be dangerous and he wanted to help Ian through it, if he could.

Everybody on board was jolted by this sharp turn. Ian had never been to this valley before and he was petrified. He was so pleased Dafydd had found him and they were together again now. Even the train hesitated. "Is there not another way?" it seemed to say, but there was no other way. The train knew it had enough momentum to carry it through this valley and on through the tunnel to the land beyond the sea. Nevertheless it was going to be a rough ride.

"Fasten your seat belts, we are expecting an uncomfortable period of our journey," an announcement said. However, earlier research had found that the combined safety risk of fitting seat belts to trains was greater than not fitting them, consequently none had been fitted (it was also the cheaper option). Hence nobody could obey the instruction.

Another voice then took over with the following announcement:

"Rejoice and be glad, we are going to visit the test track. Every aspect of the train will be tested including all the passengers. It will be great, you will travel faster than ever before, false signals will be sent to the signaling system to see what happens, extreme stress will be applied to every component to see if it cracks. Other trains don't undergo the same level of testing as the train to Zion. Previous models of the train to Zion have been here already; many of those were tested to destruction. Look over to the left and you can see the rusty remains of some of these trains. Such testing was not in vain though, a book was written about this testing which was widely published and has been studied over the last four thousand years. It contains many lessons for rail passengers and staff. It is the basis of the design of the current model that you are in today.

"Over on the right you can see a particularly interesting example of a train tested to destruction; it is called 'Bochim,' which means 'those who weep.' It was produced after the previous train 'The Son of Nun' died. 'The Son of Nun' was a fine train; it conquered many lands, and delivered a good number of its passengers to Zion. It passed every test apart from the Ai test, during which a passenger stole a vital part from the train causing it to crash. The 'Son of Nun' did not complete the whole test program; that was left to 'Bochim'.

"At this point in the history of train testing the Controller decided to allow the gremlins to remain in the valley and not drive them out straight away. A pattern then emerged, as each new train restored the honor of the company by passing a new test. The passengers then forgot about the Controller, didn't read the manual he had left for them, and the train rusted away. The Controller then sent a further model to the test track, which triumphed for a while, but eventually failed like the previous ones. Finally the Controller has sent you here."

So the train to Zion pulled into the test track reception area and everyone got off. Dr Luke met them and ushered them all into a big room where the big cheese, Professor Why (Dr Why's uncle), was to give a lecture on the purpose of testing.

LECTURE ON THE PURPOSE OF TESTING

"For nine years I have worked at this testing lab, and before that thirteen years at the national testing laboratory," he began. *"I have chaired the rail industry's testing facilities steering group for nearly ten years, so I should know something about testing by now. I have identified six main reasons why we test things in the rail industry, which I would like to share with you:*

1. *To minimize failures in service, by understanding why things go wrong which enables us to change our minds about what to do in the future.*

2. *To help produce something better; new product development involves lots of testing of prototypes before the new product is launched.*

3. *To save from death; to prevent accidents.*

4. *To reveal cracks; ultrasonic testing of rails shows up where repair work is needed.*

5. *To see if members fit together and function properly as an entity; this is called integration testing.*

6. *To validate theory; to demonstrate, in the real world, that the doctrine expounded by the rail experts is true in practice."*

"I would also like to say a few words about stress," continued Professor Why. "In metallurgy there is something called 'work hardening'. Stress is applied to a metal, which makes it tougher. In composite materials the resin, which is full of defects, entanglements, and loose ends, is only able to function usefully because of the fibers embedded within it that strengthen the whole composite structure. The stress is transferred from the resin, the weak member of the structure, onto the strong stiff fibers, which I think are divine, but some others I know consider them to be a cancer risk. The interface between the resin and the fibers is crucial; the product becomes useless if the bond is broken—this can happen by slow seepage of foreign matter through capillary action or by rapid crack propagation along the interface.

"Testing demonstrates to the world, to potential passengers and skeptics alike, 'the glory of the rail system perfected in us.' And we are the 'us', the new generation of train lovers. Surely this is what happened to an announcer called Job. Eventually Job understood that the Controller had the right to create things as he saw fit, and this creative process includes testing.

"Some have had a very high calling to endure much testing, suffering at the hands of inexperienced, ignorant engineers, to demonstrate their inner power to overcome. Some, like Mr Wurmbrand, have spoken of experiencing a special presence during these times of testing. In some ways this experience can be even more marvelous than never having had any difficulties to overcome, or being mended instantly when a problem occurs.

"I can tell you that you will never be tested beyond your ability to withstand. There will always be a way to pass the test, and the power to endure will be provided to those who believe this.

"So, if suffering and testing come your way it must be that the Controller knows you can overcome, though not by relying on your own strength. The

burden he gives us is not heavy, when shared. He has promised to take all the stress as we, like the resin, transfer the stress to the super-strong carbon fiber.

"*So the valley of Achor, which means 'trouble', can become a door of hope. In fact if you look carefully at the end of the valley you can just make out a door with the word hope inscribed on it. No? I will pass round my binoculars so that you can all see.*"

When his turn came Ian could just make out the word "hope" on a door or was it "hop"? After he had passed on the binoculars, he was not quite sure what he had seen. The lecture continued:

"*We can overcome, and when we do, we will be awarded crowns for our suffering when we reach the end of the line. So, just as we can't understand how materials behave without testing them, so we can't understand trains and their components, without testing them. This is how we prove the designer's skill; through putting our faith in the train as we ride in it here at the test track, and then on the main line on the other side of the door of hope.*"

And with that discourse ringing in their ears they were off to the first test. It was the vibration test rig. Here they were shaken about with such violence that they were nearly sick, and some of the bolts started to come loose from the train. One of the frequencies hit the resonant frequency of one of the components and it rang out like a bell screaming with pain. Before long the whole train started to jump up and down, as well as side to side, even though it was not even moving. Then at last it stopped.

"What was the purpose of that?" Ian asked Dr Luke, the guide.

"That shaking was to shake everything in and on the train so that what cannot be shaken might remain." Fortunately, Ian had hung on as instructed and seemed none the worse for wear. One or two others were not looking so good though and were taken over to the site hospital. Even Professor Why was looking a bit off-color.

The next test was the soak test. The train was driven into a chamber where the temperature and humidity were increased, and everybody was then just left there to endure it. All phones were taken away, and there were no announcements, so all means of communication were removed. Access to the testing manual was denied during this test. Some fainted, some cried out to be let off the train, and others started shouting at each other and cursing the Controller who had permitted this test to be carried out. However, there was a place of rest on the train, where you could get relief, where there was a cool refreshing breeze and fresh ice-cold water to drink, but not everyone found this secret chamber as, at first sight, it looked even hotter and more claustrophobic than the rest of the train. Ian had found this little room because it had been pointed out to him by his cousin Dafydd, who had been there before.

The third test was out on the test track itself. The train had to do 1,000 km round the test track without failing. This was rather boring, just going round and round the same track time and time again, always the same view, no music, and no stopping for a rest. No fresh food or water was provided during this test.

At last the third test was complete and the final test commenced—the crash test. In this test the train was revved up as fast as it could go and allowed to crash into the buffers. It was a straight narrow track down a steep hill; the train would have come off the straight and narrow had the driver not had faith in both the train, and the Controller. There was a carefully designed crumple zone at the front of the train. Then smash, the train hit the buffers and the front section collapsed like a pack of cards. "Was it designed to do that?" Ian wondered. The buffers were heading towards him inside the train as everybody looked on in horror! But just before the buffers reached the passengers the train came to a halt. All had been saved. Apart from the driver. We saw the driver being carried away with a sheet over him amidst much weeping from the staff and all those around him who saw the crash. One of the staff (called Oriog) was so ashamed of the whole set up that he even denied that he worked at the test center at all when a little girl asked him why he was crying.

But to everyone's great amazement three days later reports were heard from the center's admin staff that the driver was alive again and would be out of hospital very soon. Ian could not believe it, he was sure that was it for the driver. One of his friends vaguely remembered that the driver had said not to worry if he came a cropper in this test, as he would see them on the other side. Nobody really understood this at the time.

Two of the passengers had gone for a walk to get out of the test center for a bit; it was getting too much for them. Halfway through their walk they met a stranger who seemed vaguely familiar. He asked them about the test center, what had happened there, and why they were so sad. He had a copy of the test manual with him and he started to explain to them the purpose of the various tests. They went into the café and had a tea and a lamb sandwich together (that was the driver's favorite). Then he was gone. Those two passengers ran back to the test center and said, "We think we might have seen the driver. He looked like him, although a bit altered, and he certainly knew his stuff—he explained loads of things from the test manual that we had struggled to understand before."

Then eleven passengers went upstairs to have a think. They locked the door. Then there he was, the driver, looking as right as rain. He spoke to them, showed his wounds, and asked them if they now believed him. Wow! Wonder of Wonders! It *was* him, come back to life again and ready to drive through the door of hope on the next phase of the journey to Zion.

Chapter 27

The Railway Children

Just after departing from the test track, Ian was looking out of the window and caught a glimpse of a little girl on her mother's shoulders, looking down at the train to Zion.

"Look," he said to Dafydd, who was sitting next to him, making sure Ian was recovering well from the shock of the visit to the test track. Dafydd had also comforted Matthieu and Charles who had looked a bit shaken too.

A second pair of young eyes was also straining to see over the bridge as the train passed by underneath. The sisters were beaming with joy at the sight of the train.

The next station was not far and Ian was delighted to see this little family get on the train and sit down opposite them. Each had a little bag containing books. They sat down, excitedly got out a book each, and started to read out loud. Then the older girl started singing this little song:

> *"There's two, there's four, there's six, there's eight,*
> *Shunting trucks and hauling freight.*
> *Red and green brown and blue, . . ."*[28]

"Shut up won't you," shouted a rather pompous man sitting at the other end of the carriage, trying to read his newspaper. Here were a couple of young girls having the time of their lives, obviously besotted with trains who were now looking perplexed at this outburst.

"Shouldn't let such noisy kids on our train should they Ethel?" he continued to his wife. Ethel, however, kept her peace.

Ian pondered how these girls might be when they are Ethel's age. So many children love trains when they are little, but so few (especially girls) actually join the company when they are older. Ian then remembered a much-overlooked paragraph in the great train book; it said, "Let the little children come on board." Ian thought the man at the back of the carriage had obviously never read this section, or if he had, he had considered it unimportant.

The company had just completed an initiative to try to get young girls interested in the rail industry. The workforce is only 5% female, which means that 45% of the population are not contributing to the rail system at all, which is a great loss to the company, and may explain why customer care has not been as good as it is in other industries where there is a better gender balance. Ian had read about this initiative and wanted to do something, so when this pompous man shouted at these girls to keep quiet (and it was not even a quiet carriage!), Ian was moved to take action.

Ian reached out to the little girls, who were by now starting to look upset, and gave them each a hug. He then talked to them for the next hour all about his adventures on the train to Zion, how he was given a free ticket, how he had left his friends to take the train to Zion. He told of the great hailstorm, the Controller, what the Controller's son had done, and how the crew had not always been that helpful to the passengers. The girls were enthralled. Thanks to Ian they had not been put off by this "gentle" man who wanted them to be quiet. This pleased Ian. Their mother too seemed impressed and so this little family agreed to stay on the train and not to get off at the next station as they had intended.

The girls had been told that the train to Zion was smelly, noisy, with hard seats, no toilets, and was full of unfriendly people. But now, after Ian's intervention, they were starting to see the truth; how loving and friendly the passengers really are (with one or two exceptions), and how much fun it was to ride on the train to Zion.

The youngest girl had two copies of *Thomas the Tank Engine* in her bag, both presents from aunts last Christmas. This little girl took one of these precious books from her bag and said to Ian, "Here I want you to have this; I can see you love trains and I have two of these, would you like to keep this for yourself?"

Ian was a little overwhelmed, a tear almost formed in his eye. "Oh yes, thank you so much," he said. Ian promised to carry this book with him on the rest of his journey all the way to Zion.

A little victory had been won today thought Ian. The love he was able to express had overcome the pomposity of the man at the back of the carriage, the little girl had learnt to be generous, and the man at the back of the carriage had learnt to shut up and listen.

"Well done," said Dafydd to Ian. Dafydd was so happy that his cousin was now spreading the good news about the train to Zion, just as he had done in Bhutan.

Chapter 28

The Board Meeting

THE TRAIN WAS NOW heading towards Clapham Junction, where there was a conference center for rail staff. Somehow rail staff always seem to get the most convenient sites for their offices, right next to major stations. It was here that the company board meeting was to take place and Ian had been invited to attend as an observer.

The Controller's son had appointed twelve members to the board of the Rail Company. They were to carry on the good work he had started. They were a motley crew, a doctor, several fishermen, a tax collector, and two Judes. One Jude was appointed finance director even though he was suspected of embezzlement, the other was Jude Thaddaeus (related to James Mercy-Over-Judgment).

Each year there was supposed to be a board dinner. That is when they were due to remember their origins (a de-merger from an overly aggressive company based in Coventry) and how they were saved from a series of disasters including a river turning red, and the worst ever hail storm. They were to remember how their first managing director led them out of that situation to form a new company with a new constitution. Every year they should have held this dinner but times had been hard and it was often forgotten, or replaced with other less somber events celebrating non-rail matters.

This year, however, Oriog and John Four had booked a room for thirteen and had prepared everything as instructed. However, Jude was plotting a boardroom coup. He had met with senior managers from another company who had agreed to pay him a good sum of money if he could get rid of the current managing director (the Controller's son) and hand the company over to them.

The Controller's son gave the after dinner speech. From the tone of his speech it sounded very much like this was going to be his last dinner (or "supper" as this annual event had quaintly become known). He talked about how he had given himself, body and blood, for the company, for their passengers, and in fact for everybody (because everybody was entitled to travel on the train to Zion; he had ensured that). But then he said, "Look, one of you round this table is betraying me."

You can imagine the stunned silence at this claim. Then the twelve started talking amongst themselves, ignoring the managing director, trying to figure out who might be betraying the company. Some of them realized there might soon be a vacancy at the top, so they started to argue about who was the best director, who had the best reputation (and thus who might take over if a vacancy did arise).

Jude had just dipped his bread in a bowl of sauce at the same time as the Controller's son. Then the Controller's son continued: "He who dipped his bread in this bowl with me is the one who is going to betray me."

"Surely you don't mean me!" exclaimed Jude.

"You said it," the Controller's son replied.

Then the Controller's son did a very strange thing. It had been raining outside and the path to the room where they were having their meal was muddy. Everyone's shoes were filthy and there was a bad smell too. The path was often used by dog walkers and some people had brought in evidence of that on their shoes. Nobody had said anything, but at this point the Controller's son left the table, changed into overalls, went to a cupboard marked "slippers," and got out twelve pairs of beautiful crimson slippers. He then removed the muddy shoes from all the guests and replaced them with the new slippers he had provided. He then returned to his place.

Then at the end of the meal they sang the company song and went to a nearby hill to gaze at the stars; it was a magnificent night, they could see all the glory of the night sky, from Andromeda to the Crab Nebula, and even the Super Nova that had burst forth 33 years ago, (though it was now fading from sight to the unaided eye).

Jude had slipped away from them almost unnoticed, but he reappeared with about twenty armed soldiers in military uniform and a group of men dressed in very smart suits; these were directors from the company that Jude had made the deal with. Jude went up to the Controller's son and gave him the traditional greeting. This was the pre-arranged sign so they would know who the Controller's son was. At this signal the solders grabbed the Controller's son but Oriog took out his flick-knife and instinctively threw it at one of the soldiers, before he could think through the consequences of his action. It hit the soldier on the ear. "I am so sorry about that," apologized the Controller's son on Oriog's behalf and then bandaged up the wound.

Then the soldiers took away the Controller's son and all the company board members went their separate ways. The boardroom coup was complete.

The next morning Jude woke up with the fee for his treachery under his pillow. To keep the arrangement secret they had paid him in cash. Jude had not slept well. Not only was the cash making his pillow hard, but his heart had become hard too. He realized the terrible mistake he had made. He had betrayed the company and he had betrayed his good friend who had trusted him to be finance director despite knowing his past conviction for embezzlement. He had not expected it to turn violent like this. So he decided to return the cash. He went to the offices of the new company and, in a fit of remorse, threw all the cash into the reception area from where it floated up to the vast ceiling blown there by the state of the art air conditioning system designed to remove the bad odors from the feet of the directors of the company.

Out stormed Jude. He had had enough. He had had enough of trains, enough of finance, enough of boardroom fights, enough of striving to be the best. He had had enough of life. He walked all the way to Clapham Junction in the rain, he forced his way through the gate with such force that it snapped. He ran up the stairs, smashed the little window over platform 22 on the bridge over the tracks and hurled himself over the edge directly in front of the 16.27 to Woking.

All the trains in the South East of England stopped. His body was taken to Mortlake and cremated. The new company called a board meeting. The first item on the agenda was what to do with the cash Jude had returned to them. They couldn't just put it through their accounts they realized, as questions would be asked by the auditors. "Perhaps we could buy the potter's field," one of them suggested. "The field next to the conference center in Clapham Common; we could turn it into a garden of remembrance for all those who have committed suicide on rail lines." They all agreed that this was the best thing to do with Jude's blood money.

As they were preparing for the opening of this garden, they discovered an old stone encryption, which they decided to display as the centerpiece of the garden of remembrance. It read:

> "*After the original train crew caused so many deaths the Controller will remove these drivers, announcers, and cleaners, and replace them with his own son. But he will be betrayed for the price of this field and the blood of the betrayer will be poured out next to this field. This land will never be built on and the director's role that becomes vacant as a result must be filled again with one better than he.*"

And so it happened that Jude was replaced by Matt when the company board was re-established after the death of the Controller's son. Two applications were received for Jude's post and this was the last time that the toss of a coin was used to decide on a board position.

What extraordinary board meetings, Ian thought to himself. Then the directors headed back to the train with Matt appointed as the new finance director, leaving behind a garden of remembrance hidden behind some trees at the far end of Clapham Common.

Chapter 29

The Controller's Son Comes to Town

BIDDING FAREWELL TO CLAPHAM Junction and the members of the Rail Board, Ian returned to his seat but he could not settle down after all the events he had just witnessed. Instead he set off to walk along the entire train just to see what he could see. Suddenly he was full of the joys of spring, even though it was now autumn, as he enjoyed the scenes of English oak leaves falling to the ground, neatly mowed cricket squares being covered for the winter, garden barbeques being put away for the season, and the last of the year's country fetes whizzing past him.

He expected to find his cousin Dafydd, but he was nowhere to be seen. Before he could make much progress, the train came to a halt at Herodium, where there was an old run-down chapel, which looked to Ian like the Talybont Bethlehem Chapel he had known as a young boy. He spotted a group of people looking at a new poster that had just been posted outside the station waiting room.

> *Coming of Age of the Controller's son*
> *42nd generation celebration on Sunday at*
> *Kefar Nahum, 10 am.*
> *All welcome!*

He got off the train to find out what all the fuss was about, having checked when the train would set off again.

One man in the crowd (Andrew Jones was his name) was reading the poster and said, with an accent that warmed Ian's heart, "I heard he is worth listening to."

Another of Ian's countrymen (Oriog Jones was his name) replied, "Yes I am going to go; I heard he can turn water into wine; that should be worth seeing." This was the same Oriog Jones that had worked at the Test Centre and had arranged the famous Clapham Junction board meeting.

Ian too had heard a lot of rumors about the Controller's son but wasn't sure about them, so he reasoned this would be a good opportunity to find out the truth.

So the following Sunday Ian made his way from Herodium to Kefar Nahum. There was a big crowd assembled at the station to welcome the Controller's son off the 10.00 from Herodium. The leaflet for the event said he would be dressed in a bright red military uniform carrying a sword and a trumpet, so you couldn't miss him. When the station clock struck ten (Bristol time) the train arrived, bang on time. The crowd pushed forward to where the front of the train would stop, where the first class carriage would be.

Out stepped Major Maccabees an elderly gentleman dressed in a red military uniform (it couldn't be him though—too old), then an unshaven young announcer (John Grace Make-Ready) wearing a goat-skin coat and carrying a magazine about the nutritional value of insects, (Ian had met him earlier, surely it was not him), and finally a very beautiful young lady called Myriam, dressed in blue, smiling broadly at all the attention.

Meanwhile the Controller's son had emerged unnoticed from the rear of the train dressed like everyone else in standard class. He then approached the barrier that had been erected to control the crowd and spoke to the security guard. He showed his ticket and his passport.

"Where have you come from?" the guard snapped—he had yet to attend the "customer care +" training course in Milton Keynes.

"En-Nasirah," he replied, even though his passport showed his place of birth to be near Herodium.

"Can anything good come out of En-Nasirah!" he joked, as the place had a reputation somewhat like Slough or Wapping. The guard looked at his list of expected guests to welcome the Controller's son and none was from En-Nasirah.

"You will have to go over there," he said pointing to a cow shed in a field adjacent to the station, where a small group of the uninvited had gathered to see if they could catch a glimpse of the arrival of the Controller's son.

So, as instructed, the Controller's son made his way to the field. The cows used to wait by the gate for the farmer to feed them and so the entrance into the field from the station was particularly muddy. It had been raining, so by the time the Controller's son arrived at the cowshed the bottom of his white trousers were a dark shade of brown. Undeterred, he started talking to those who were there.

Here are some of the things he said:

- "Give and it shall be given to you."[29]

- "Love your neighbor as yourself."[30]

- "The day of rest was made for you; you were not made for the day of rest."

- "Give to the King what belongs to the King and to the Controller what belongs to him."

- "Eat my body and drink my blood which is poured out so that everyone can find forgiveness."

The crowd were amazed.

Then he asked if anyone was ill. Someone (Oriog Jones) shouted from the back, "My mother-in-law has not been feeling too well!" And his mates next to him remarked "She's been off-color ever since she set eyes on you!"

"Where does she live?"

"Third house on the left above the baker's, just the other side of that gate."

At that the Controller's son walked straight for "that gate," and despite the cows' attempts to discourage him, he untied the gate and walked over to the third house on the left, rang the bell, and disappeared into the house. The crowd followed to see what would happen. A few minutes later the Controller's son re-emerged with the mother-in-law who looked as right as rain.

"She was at death's door this morning, I swear," said Oriog, the son-in-law.

Next a man covered all over in running sores approached the Controller's son.

"I have been ill with these terrible sores for years. Nobody will touch me because they are so infectious," he said.

The crowd took a step back, leaving just the Controller's son to talk to him alone.

"Please heal me, please," he said. "You can do it, I know. Will you?" The Controller's son felt sorry for him; in fact he felt more than just sorrow, he wanted to do something special for him. So he reached out his hand and touched him (nobody had done that since he had been diagnosed). It was an expression of friendship that really moved him. Not only that, the Controller's son also said, "I will, be cleansed," and the man was. All the sores were healed in an instant.

The crowd were even more amazed now.

Then it started to rain, and before long it was chucking it down. The cow shed was empty of cows because they had been taken to new pasture in the next field. It was a big herd so the shed was big enough for the whole crowd to shelter in. They wanted to find out more about this extraordinary man (they still had not worked out who he was). So they all packed into the cowshed and asked the Controller's son to come with them and say a few more words. He was happy to oblige.

Word had spread fast through the town about what had happened to the mother-in-law and the man with the sores; both were well known in the town. So what had been a relatively small crowd huddled together in the cowshed, had now grown to fill the entire field. (The crowd at the station waiting for the arrival of the Controller's son had diminished by now.)

"Mind your backs, mind your backs," shouted four Saint John Ambulance cadets. (The Jones brothers, Andrew, who was a good listener, and Oriog who was a good talker, both fishermen; Mary Alabaster Rahab, a fit young lady with a strong character, and her training partner Samaria Potleft). They were carrying a friend on a stretcher because he was unable to walk. He had been paralyzed in a motorbike accident last year (the other driver had died). He had asked his friends to take him to see this person who had healed the mother-in-law and the man with the sores. His name was "Benderfynol o Ffydd," which means "Determined Faith" in English. So they made their way to the cowshed, but they could not get in as it was so packed.

"I have got an idea," said one of the four. He was always having bright ideas, sometimes crazy, sometimes brilliant; he was never one to accept defeat. This was Oriog Jones down to a tee.

"Look there are some steps round the back." So they clambered up the steps with their paralyzed friend clinging on for dear life. When they got to the top they couldn't see a thing. It was still raining and it looked like the bright spark of the four was going to have to accept defeat this time, but no . . .

"I've got another idea," Oriog said, his three friends looking on apprehensively and by now soaked to the skin.

"Let's remove a bit of this corrugated roof and lower him down that way!"

"You're crazy, we could all fall and injure ourselves and then we would be paralyzed too!" complained one of the four, but despite the obvious risk and the discouragement just expressed, they decided to give it a go.

Down below nobody could hear what the Controller's son was saying because of the rain on the roof and the noise of the roof panel being removed by the St John Ambulance cadets. Then the crowd inside saw the stretcher lowered down in front of them, right next to the Controller's son.

What was he going to say? What would he do now?

The Controller's son then announced in a loud voice, "Forget about the accident, even though it was your fault, you are forgiven."

"You are not a judge, you can't pass sentence just like that, there has to be a trial and a jury, and all the evidence has to be carefully weighed up before he can be let off," shouted the brother of the one who had died in the motorbike accident last year.

"Actually I am a judge and I do have authority to declare forgiveness," and with that he said to the paralyzed man: "Get up and take your stretcher with you, go home, and have a bath."

More amazement as, in front of the crowd, the paralyzed man stood up, put the stretcher under his arm and walked out of the cow shed.

"We have never seen anything like this!" the crowd said to each other.

After this, over the next three years, the Controller's son did many things like that and taught many amazing things too. Everybody in the country had heard about him; he could no longer travel incognito in the back of the train like he did that day.

But people didn't know what to make of him. He wasn't what they were expecting. There were many different reactions to him. After his death, some did start their journey to Zion on the train but many others who were already on the train decided not to get back on the train to Zion. Ian however did return to his seat, along with a journalist called Jean-Luc who put together this summary of what had happened when the Controller's son came to town:

"I have undertaken to compile an account of the things that have taken place amongst us about which there is firm evidence. I have been given eyewitness accounts. Other reliable sources, which I can vouch for, have provided me with further information. It seemed fitting to me to investigate everything very carefully right from the beginning and write out in consecutive order what happened so that you might know the truth. In this article I summarize the reactions of those who saw and heard the Controller's son, the 42nd generation of that illustrious Davidson family:

1. Some *followed* him (only twelve people followed him for the full three years and one of these betrayed him in the end and then committed suicide).

2. Big crowds *gathered together to hear him* (whole cities, five thousand families on one occasion on top of a hill, multitudes were drawn to see him heal people).

3. Some *walked away* from him when they heard difficult sayings that they didn't understand, (e.g. the one about eating his flesh and drinking his blood).

4. Some *went out of their way* to see him (a short man called Zach climbed a tree to be able to see him, a lady with a flow of blood pushed through the crowd so that she could just touch his coat).

5. Some responded to him by obeying his instructions to *go heal the sick* and *bring good news* to nearby towns (72 people did this on one occasion).

6. Some *followed him secretly* (there was one senior civil servant who was a secret follower; he was the one who paid for his burial).

7. Some *were skeptical* (particularly the lawyers and academics—they had a very specific expectation of what sort of person he should be and when he turned out differently they asked him lots of trick questions and eventually turned against him).

8. Some *thought he was not the Controller's son* but just an announcer like many other announcers before him, though a very good announcer at that. A growing number believed that the Controller could not have a son.

9. Some *despised and rejected* him.

10. Some *stood at a distance* intrigued but fearful.

11. Some saw many amazing things but still *doubted* (one person, Thomas Doubtful, was well known for this).

12. Some *shouted 'kill him.'*

13. Some *sentenced him to death* under pressure from the crowd and said they washed their hands of their responsibility.

14. Some actually *killed him* (though one of these realized who he was during the execution).

15. Some *went to be with him* in paradise after he died (including a thief who was being executed at the same time as him).

16. Many *saw him alive again* after he had died (one reliable account mentioned 500 people and most of these eyewitnesses are still alive today. If you want to track them down yourself and question them about this you still can).

17. Some *believed in him* so much they were prepared to die. (One of his followers was stoned to death for his beliefs, Stephen Martyr was his name, and he was the first of many stretching right to the present time).

18. Some *were lukewarm* about him. (A particular group from a place called Laodicea were well known for this).

19. Some *said they believed* everything they heard about him *but did nothing* about it. (One reporter, James was his name, said this could not have been true belief because if it were true faith, it would have resulted in action).

20. Some *loved him* at first but abandoned their first love (a particular group from a place called Ephesus were well known for this; but they were offered a second chance if they remembered from where they had fallen, turned back, and did again the things they had done when they first followed him).

"These are written that you may believe that he was the son of the Controller and that by believing you may have life in his name.

"I was one of the twelve followers with him for the last three years of his life, I have testified to these events, I have recorded them here and it is well known that this account of these things is accurate. There were very many other things that the Controller's son did. If all these were written in detail in books and spread out over the earth's entire surface there would still be many books left over. This is just a summary of some of the things he did and some of the reactions people had to him. If you want to know more ask him yourself—he is not dead, he is risen from the dead and will keep his promise that he who keeps on asking him will receive, he who keeps on seeking him will find, he who keeps on knocking at his door it will be opened to him, and that door is the door to the train to Zion which is still being opened for any who wish to be with him forever. But the door will close when you lie down to die."

After Ian had read Jean-Luc's article, he carefully folded it up and placed it in his bag so that he could pass this remarkable record on to future generations.

Chapter 30

The Train Stops

BACK ON THE TRAIN again, with the visit of the Controller's son still fresh in his mind, Ian sat down next to the window and took in the view as the train sped happily along through the English countryside towards the south coast, where the train line disappeared into a tunnel under the sea. The golden autumn colors of Kentish vineyards and hop fields warmed his soul. Ian was feeling happy, pleased to have finally met the Controller's son and now safely on the train to Zion. However, in a dark corner of his soul there lurked a residue of anxiety about the tunnel ahead. Matthieu and Charles who had remained in their seats in Ian's carriage were also looking apprehensive.

Across the aisle an earnest conversation had started between a vicar, a farmer, a doctor and his old friend Professor Demas, the rail engineer, concerning the exact nature of the train they were on.

Then suddenly the train came to a halt in the middle of nowhere. After about half an hour of perplexity Ian became a bit impatient with the delay and started to wonder why the train had stopped. Just then an announcement came over the tannoy apologizing for the delay—there appeared to be a signaling problem. Across the aisle from Ian the four friends restarted their discussion, getting louder and louder every second so that before long the whole carriage could hear what they were saying. Everybody in the carriage was following the conversation, which was obviously very important.

This is what Professor Demas said: "There seem to me to be five possible reasons why this train has stopped."

"Firstly, it could be frozen switches/points, unlikely to be ice as the temperature is too warm for that, but it could be other gunk clogging up the switches/points.

"Secondly," he continued with an air of a college lecturer, "it could be a problem with data transfer. The original message telling the train what to do may not be getting through.

"Thirdly, the original message could be being changed as it gets transmitted from the originator to the tracks where the train is now.

"Fourthly, it could be a spurious signal which is dominating so much that the correct signal, though still there, is drowned out. In this case I would expect the train to fail-safe, i.e. stop because it has not received a clear message on how to proceed.

"Finally, it could be a fault with this bit of the track, for example the foundations here could be suspect, or the drainage poor."

Having concluded his mini-lecture the professor stopped talking and the farmer who Ian had not met before, a Mr Angus Buchan, offered these thoughts:

"Let me tell you how I see this from my experience. I am an arable farmer. I plant seed in my soil and expect to see the fruit of my labors before the end of the season. I can then use some of the seed for sowing the next crop, some to feed my family, and the rest we can sell to pay for things we need. Your message, Professor, your data, is like the DNA of my seed. Perhaps you rail engineers can learn from nature about how signals are transmitted and why there are often issues. My experience might just help you understand why the train has stopped.

"I have four types of soil on my farm and just one type of seed. The seed is good and it contains the entire DNA necessary for it to multiply a hundred-fold. Each new seed contains the same DNA message as the original. I scatter the seed in all types of soil; I don't like to judge which is good ground and which is not. Sometimes the seed falls on the path, birds then come and eat it up and so my farm sees no crop from this ground at all. When the seed falls on rocky ground, it germinates fine but then wilts because its roots are poor and it can't stand the heat of the sun. Other seed falls among thorns, where it sprouts well but is then choked by the more vigorous growth of the thorns. So the message that gets passed on to the next generation in this field is one of thorns, not good plants. This, Professor, is a bit like your fourth type of signal failure when the good message gets replaced with a wrong message. But some seed falls into good soil where it grows well and produces a hundred more seeds, all with the same message inside, able to reproduce themselves, not sterile like some GM seeds that greedy suppliers sell that give a good crop in the first season but then fail to reproduce at all.

"So as this train is stuck, going nowhere, why not ponder a while more on my business of farming and you might learn how to get the train moving again?

"To get a good crop you need good seed, good soil, water, and sunshine. Good soil is actually produced from failures, dead plants from previous years. Rotten weeds can produce great compost, much better than sterile sand. Life seems to come from death, the hundred-fold multiplication of the message is aided by this compost made from plants that seemed like a complete waste, but actually such organic material is an essential ingredient for a good soil.

"The next lesson is about dispersal. If all the seed from one plant just drops next to the original plant the hundred little plants trying to grow would crowd each other out and few, if any, would reach maturity. In the wild however, wind comes and blows the seed into fresh soil where new plants can flourish. In a cultivated field we cut down the plant and separate the wheat from the chaff. We plant the seed in the soil so the next generation can continue and its DNA is preserved.

"My next lesson is about reproduction. Plants are sexual beings. Bees, or other insects, are needed to join the male cells to the female cells. The beauty is enhanced over the years as their flowers become more and more attractive to the bees. If you just had white and red flowers, the plant world would be unattractive to both bees and people compared to all the pinks and varieties of color you see in today's flowers. So there is a certain beauty and practical benefit from diversity. There is also a need for bees to bring together diverse parts of the species. The bees need to be rewarded too, with nectar for themselves and their families.

"One final lesson from me and then I will let someone else have their say. Farming has seasons; you need to plant the seed at the right time when the soil is receptive, warm, and just before the first rains. Then you have to wait for the plants to grow, wait for the sun and the rain to mature the plants over the summer when sweetness is produced in the form of sugar in the fruit around the seed ready for the next generation. Having persevered through storms, plagues, drought, and floods, finally autumn comes and the message can be passed on in the seed within the fruit."

The doctor was next to speak.

"Thank you for your insights, Mr Buchan, I am reminded that human cells are rather like plant seeds, they too reproduce after their own kind when the conditions are right. However, we are this afternoon looking to understand what has gone wrong with the signaling system. Let me offer my insight from my specialism. My job is to treat cancer. A cancerous cell is one that carries a false message in its DNA and reproduces this error in the next generation of cells. The worst cancers are those that grow up unnoticed, like BSE, and have very long incubation times. They sap the strength away from normal cells, reducing the ability of the normal cells to reproduce their DNA with the correct embedded message. Cancer prevents normal growth of the body. Eventually it kills the body, or worse still it infects the next generation, so that the deadly message in the DNA contaminates future generations and eventually the whole species.

"Early diagnosis of cancer is key. Cancerous cells that are very different from true cells are easy to spot and deal with. The problem is with cells that look like all the rest on the outside but have a false heart. To detect an early cancer you need, within the body, cells with the power to discern the difference between true cells and false ones. Next you need to communicate this information to the rest of the body so that action can be taken to kill the cancer, to separate it from the body as far as the east is from the west. Where the body tolerates a cancer, taking no action, the cancerous cells will multiply and grow strong. It will be very difficult to remove the cancer without damaging the rest of the body.

"Cancerous cells are a bit like your seeds of weeds, Mr Buchan, they grow up alongside true plants, but they don't produce the right fruit or the right seeds. They weaken the other plants by taking their sustenance, crowding them out. Cancerous cells, like weeds, are also defined by their context; dandelions growing on a lawn are weeds but if you want to produce a dandelion and burdock drink, a field of dandelions is just what you want. In the same way if cells in the body start to reproduce eye cells in the liver this would be called cancer and would be damaging to the body as a whole, but eye cells reproducing eye cells in the eye is just what you want.

"Within the body you need all different types of cells and members, but they need to be growing in the right place, relating well to each other, and taking instructions from the head. If a left foot decided to walk on but the right foot decided to stay put, the body would fall over and injure itself. The body needs nerve cells that communicate messages accurately from the head to the members, e.g. to feet so that the body can walk, but if the whole body was made of nerve cells the body would not be able to walk, or see or hear or do anything really. Diversity is inherent in the design of the body, but each different member needs to hear the message correctly from the head, transmitted through the nerves and relate properly with adjacent cells and members."

After contemplating these things in silence for at least twenty minutes, the vicar finally spoke.

"What you say reminds me of my job in the body of Christ, the Church. I feel I am a bit like the nerve cells seeking to communicate, honestly and sincerely, messages from the head—Jesus Christ himself, not the archbishop or the Queen you understand; I do not hold with antidisestablishmentarianism. In my time, I have seen false teaching come into the Church and weaken it like a cancer or like the weeds growing in a wheat field that produces no wheat, no seeds for sowing or flour for eating.

"I have seen whole churches frozen by not responding to the true messages they receive each week. I have seen churches where the people were eager to hear the message but the messenger, usually a vicar I am sad to say, was unable to hear from God and pass it on to the people in a way they could understand. I have seen churches where the original message was changed, so that the people got confused and gave up. I have seen churches stop functioning when the true signal is drowned out by other signals like immorality in the clergy, grumbling by the congregation over trivial matters like which songs to sing or what you should wear. I have also seen churches built on wrong foundations, not built on the revelation of Jesus as the Christ, the Messiah, the Son of God, but on well-meaning but fallible individuals; Saint Peter's in the town next to where I come from is a good example of this.

"I have also seen successful managing directors taking the place of Christ on parochial church councils thereby destroying the work of the Spirit. I have seen splits in the body of Christ over whether or not to eat Halal meat. I have seen churches stop dead in their tracks when a vicar leaves for a new church as the members were only connected to the head through signals coming via the vicar for half an hour on a Sunday morning.

"These 'leaves on the line' in the church can lead to slow running, slippage or even a crash. Despite knowing that these leaves fall each autumn, nobody seems to read the Controller's book on how to deal with them when they arrive. So when this happens we just tend to change the timetable, accept delays, and even the occasional accident. Pity really, I am sure before I retired I saw some promising solutions to this problem.

"The train to Zion was due to arrive at its destination within a generation of the new signal being installed, but nearly two thousand years later the train is still stuck or possibly moving so slowly you can't notice it actually moving at all."

Although Ian was fascinated to overhear the conversation of the engineer, the farmer, the doctor, and the vicar, he decided to get up from his seat to investigate so that he could work out for himself why the train had stopped.

Chapter 31

The Channel Tunnel to Grund

BUT BEFORE IAN HAD time to work out why the train had stopped for so long, it suddenly started moving again. The time had finally arrived. The train to Zion had reached the end of the United Kingdom. To progress further towards Zion the only option was to face the great tunnel under the sea. Passengers seated on the south side of the train could see the sea now. Some were looking forward to reaching France but others were having second thoughts, including Matthieu and Charles, as they were fearful of the tunnel, and were even wondering if France actually existed at all.

They were about to find out.

Others who had decided they did not want to go to Zion looked on as the train to Zion sped by, wondering if they had made the right decision not to board the train.

But just before the entrance to the tunnel at Folkestone the train made an unexpected stop at Sanding. There a train to Babylon drew up alongside the train to Zion. Despite the grime on the windows of that train and the smoke inside, Ian could see into the carriages and make out something of what was happening inside. There was a woman clothed in purple and scarlet, with dozens of solid gold rings on her wrists, and rubies and pearls everywhere in her hair. She was serving wine from a gold cup, to those on board. They were addicted to this wine, and were already drunk and vomiting from it, but she just carried on serving the wine to them, and they carried on drinking it.

On her forehead she had a strange tattoo; it read: "Babylon the great, the mother of harlots and the abominations of the earth."[31]

Ian gasped at the sight of her—nearly fainting in fact. She had her own cup to drink from. The liquid in her cup was not wine though. It was red; red as blood, blood extracted from the dying bodies of faithful members of the company who had spoken the words of the Controller to her and her followers, with compassion; yet their blood was her drink. She was drunk with this blood.

She had intoxicated all the nations of the earth. There were, in her train, people from every nation, tribe, and tongue, (just as there would be in the train to Zion). Presidents, Prime Ministers, and kings had visited her bedroom and every company had made their profits from her wine. Very few could live without her. Only those on the train to Zion had any chance.

The two trains were in touching distance of each other now. Ian cried out to those on the other train to get off, but they just laughed at him and carried on with their queen. Ian's voice was the last any of them were to hear because shortly after that final warning Ian's train left this tiny station and the train to Babylon veered away from the train to Zion, derailed, and tumbled down a great ravine. Ian saw the smoke rise from the abyss despite the tears in his eyes.

Those on the train to Babylon had had every opportunity to transfer to the train to Zion, many, many different opportunities (the station outside Folkestone was their final chance) but most had refused to leave their train. Now, however, the deceiving woman in purple and scarlet was dead, she would no longer be able to drink the blood of those seeking Zion, her tempting schemes were over, and her blasphemies ceased.

Once those on the train to Zion realized the significance of what had happened to their great enemy, the Controller's voice came over the tannoy saying that it is OK to be glad at her demise. For thousands of years she had fought against the Controller and now it was all over. At last the wedding of the Controller's son could happen. All in the train to Zion were invited to the wedding feast. Slowly, but profoundly, the whole train started to sing. Some realized they would soon see their loved ones again, those who had died at the hand of the lady in purple and scarlet. Some realized they had no cause to fear anymore, some were simply pleased that justice had been done, and others were happy that there would be no more obstacles on the way to Zion, no more crying, no more mourning, no more pain on the other side of the tunnel.

Ian wondered what had become of his friends Gareth, Methedig, and Nick. They had left the train to Zion. Was there any way back for them?

Was their fate the same as those on the train to Babylon? Was there another chance for them? Ian shed a tear for each of his lost friends.

Then Ian had a sudden panic about his cousin Dafydd. Where was he? He was not in Ian's carriage; he hadn't seen him since their meeting with the railway children. What about Charles, Matthieu, and Oriog? And what about all those back in Talybont that he had left behind to catch the train to Zion? They had all been offered a free ticket to Zion, but none had accepted. Should Ian have forced them to come with him? These thoughts produced a great sadness in Ian's heart. All Ian could do now was to offer up a prayer for them and trust the Controller of all the earth to do justice.

The train to Zion then pulled into a red and gold depot, sparkling clean in the golden autumn sunlight. The train was being refurbished for the last time, ready for the wedding. Everybody from the train was given new clothes, bright red suits washed clean with the blood of their savior the Controller's son. All the testing had now run its course; the train and the passengers had made themselves ready for the wedding. They were like refined silver that had been heated in the furnace over and over again to remove the dross, and they were now ready. The bride at last was ready.

It was thus with a great sense of anticipation and longing to be at last in France that the passengers in the train to Zion reached Folkestone and entered the Channel Tunnel. Though they had peace and a joy deep down, it was mixed with sadness for all those they were leaving behind.

Many other trains had gone that way before, but none had ever returned. Many of the passengers on the other trains were fearful, terrified of the tunnel and what lay beyond. Some said there was nothingness on the other side. Others said they would re-emerge in England again but in a different form. Many had not even thought about it, being intoxicated by one of the many tempting wines offered by the lady in purple and scarlet. Others had tried to avoid the tunnel altogether by not traveling by train at all, some had tried ships, aircraft and a few had tried to swim across, but none had ever returned to say what had happened to them. None of these had wanted to go to Zion, and they had got what they wanted. They were separated forever from Zion; there was no way for them to get on the train to Zion now. The doors had finally been locked, the train was off, diving below the waves into the darkness with no light visible at the end of the tunnel.

After 35 minutes the train to Zion emerged on the other side. After the darkness of the tunnel, the brightness was quite stunning.

Ian looked back momentarily. He saw a great white bird with keys in its beak and a chain in its claws. It bound the entrance from the tunnel shut. Ian also thought he saw something move in the tunnel. A slithering mass of serpent appeared, glanced at Ian with one last attempt to frighten him, but it could not get out, and Ian was no longer afraid. The serpent was kept at bay by the chain and the lock, which Ian thought were so strong they could last a thousand years.

Just as they were arriving at Calais, Ian was surprised to see another train approach. It was painted red with gold just like the train he was in. It stopped at the platform right next to Ian. Ian could see two large chairs on the platform. They were thrones in fact and they too were made of gold. People were passing by these thrones and with great joy were entering the other red and gold train. Ian recognized John Wycliffe, Dietrich Bonhoeffer, and Perpetua Felicitas. John had been killed in an accident as he had repaired the track; Dietrich had been sentenced to death because he would not drink the wine from the lady in purple and scarlet; and Perpetua had refused to have the queen of Babylon's tattoo on her forehead, which meant she could not buy or sell anything, and had starved to death. They were all made alive again though. This must be the martyr's train, Ian thought. It too was heading for Zion. There were 144,000 on this train.

They were in Calais now, though not yet in Zion. They had been through the first tunnel. All their difficulties and trials were now behind them, left on the other side of the channel, no more crying, no more mourning, no more pain. What a journey they were going to have from Calais to Zion! The Controller himself was on board now. He had come on board for the wedding of his son. The bride and the bridegroom had just got married, and Ian's train was taking them on honeymoon.

But before they set off, a precious book was opened. It was a book belonging to the Controller and he had paid a very high price to obtain it. It contained a list of names and nothing else. The title of the book was simply *The Book of Life*. Everyone on the train had to show their ticket. A machine read the magnetic strip on the ticket, decoding the record that revealed the name of the bearer of the ticket and the one who had paid for the ticket. It was the Controller's son himself who had paid for all the valid tickets, and each ticket bearer could see that his name matched with a name written in the book of life, and so had the right to travel on to Zion.

There was quite a queue. Ian noticed that some people were shown to the left after having their ticket checked, and others to the right. Ian caught a glimpse of one person who had been shown to the left; he was very agitated, distraught, and argumentative. Ian saw the door to the left open and this man was thrown out of the train into what looked like a lake of fire. Ian suddenly felt all alone. He had been separated from all his friends, and wondered where they had all gone.

Some in the queue had lost their tickets, some tickets had got coated in dirt and didn't work first time, and some had become demagnetized by being too close to their phones. Some tickets turned out to be counterfeit; some were tickets for other trains. Ian had expected everyone that had traveled with him on the train from Wales, and those who had joined the train to Zion in England, to be permitted to continue the journey through France and on to Zion, but sadly it was not so. Some had climbed onto the train without a valid ticket, without going through the narrow gate. Some thought their parents' ticket would get them through, some thought they could bluff their way through, and others thought their own hard work for the company would mean they would be given a valid ticket in the end, but none of these people could stay on the train. Only those who had accepted the free tickets bought for them by the Controller's son, and who had kept them safe, could continue the journey.

Ian now reached the front of the queue. He reached for his ticket. Where was it? Where had he put it? He remembered he had hidden it somewhere for safekeeping. Surely he had used it to get on the train in Wales. Had he lost it?

After what seemed like an eternity, Ian finally found his ticket, next to his heart, warm and dry. He presented it with confidence, he had faith that it was valid, he had assurance that he was going to see his name in the book of life and yes, there it was! So Ian was ushered through the door to the right into an even more beautiful carriage. And there, to his astonishment, he saw his three old friends Gareth, Methedig, and Nick. What a reunion that was! They hugged each other, cried till their eyes hurt with tears of joy unspeakable. Eventually Ian asked them to tell him what had happened to them after they had left the train to Zion in England, and how they had ended up here in Calais.

Methedig got up from his seat, sat next to Ian and started to tell what had happened to them. "After we left the train to Zion we all went our separate ways. I was stuck in this care-home in Saint Margaret's. We all got lost. I was still in my wheel chair then, and one day I ended up on a train with disabled access but no disabled egress. Nobody came to help me off, it was hell. Then just as I thought I was about to die this shepherd got onto my train and said he had been looking for me everywhere. He asked me if I was sorry I had left the train to Zion. I admitted I was sorry and then he offered to carry me all the way to Folkestone, which he did. Then the Controller sent another train for me called *Amazing Grace*. It was going to Zion. So even though I did not deserve another ticket to Zion I was given one, free of charge, in exchange for my ticket to hell. Gareth and Nick were on this train too. We must have got here just before you."

"And how did you get here?" Ian asked Nick.

"Well, after I left the train to Zion during the terrorist attack, I found myself a job in the bank of Shinar. I was eventually appointed a director of the bank. It was a fabulously rich company, all due to burning fossil fuels and thereby ruining our planet. However, I was caught for insider dealing. I could not pay the fine and ended up in prison. I was feeling very lost there as you can imagine and was so pleased when a cleaning lady there spoke kindly to me. She said she could get me another ticket to Zion if I wanted one. I said, 'Yes please,' and told her how sorry I was to have left the train to Zion before. So the very next day she brought me a new ticket personally signed by the Controller's son. The prison governor called me to her office and told me my fine had been paid in full and that I was free to go. As I left the prison the cleaning lady met me and showed me the way to the station where I caught a train to Calais using my new ticket."

"Amazing! Wow!" exclaimed Ian.

"And you, Gareth, what is your story?"

"I tried to settle down near Twickenham. You remember how I loved the game of rugby, but eventually I realized how futile it was. I returned to Wales, got a job on a farm, not a lovely sheep farm on the hills of Powys, but a pig farm in Swansea. I was treated so badly. I had signed up to forego my minimum wage in exchange for my accommodation, which turned out to be a pigsty! How I longed to be with you again on the train to Zion, so I decided to leave the pig farm and offer to work as a cleaner on the train to Zion if they would have me. On the way to the interview for the cleaning job the Controller himself ran to meet me, offered me a free seat on the train *Amazing Grace*, gave me new clothes to wear, and put this gold ring on my finger. Not everyone at the interview was happy with how I got onto the train, but I was!"

Ian was about to tell his story when in stepped his cousin Dafydd. More hugs and tears of joy followed this reunion. Dafydd had been on the train to Zion all the time. He had been going from person to person singing the songs of Zion, and offering to share his thoughts on the terms and conditions of travel that the Controller had provided to all the passengers. Some had listened and they remained on the train, but other refused and they were among the ones who had left the train never to return. Dafydd had done all he could for his fellow passengers, even at the cost of not being with his cousin Ian for so long. But now they were reunited and Ian was able to tell the four of them all about his adventures since he had last seen them.

But there was no sign of Matthieu and Charles.

After Ian had finished telling what had happened to him, a man dressed all in white entered their carriage and said, "Give me your bottle." This was a special bottle that Ian had been given by Ab and in it Ian had collected all his tears. "You have no need of that anymore."

"Here, take this white stone," the man dressed in white said. "It has your name written on it." It was a precious present to Ian. He kept it next to his heart.

Ian sat by an open window next to his friends and his cousin as the train moved off into France. He observed the new vista that opened up before him and felt the gentle wind of the pure fresh air against his face. He had never been outside the UK, none of the passengers with him, apart from Dafydd, had been abroad either, so it was all new. They could see springs of fresh water, lakes as clear as crystal, reflecting the glory and warmth of the sun, and a group of little trees growing next to a stream. Everything seemed different; it was like seeing in color after only having a black and white TV, or like seeing in three dimensions after only being able to see in two before. It was out of this world. Ian was so happy.

Soon he was talking excitedly with people he knew, who had died long ago. He also talked with some of the great heroes of the past; Zech, Jake, and Ab told him their life stories during the first month of the journey through Europe, and Ian was over the moon.

After many happy days traveling across the flat plains of northern France, the incline started to get steeper and then steeper still. The view out of the window changed from lush meadows to mountain streams and then arid bare peaks. There were dry valleys everywhere. Surely this was not the way to Zion. The train stopped. A crowd had gathered on the platform. Some on the platform wore sheepskin coats, for it was cold at this altitude; others wore black and white prayer shawls.

"Which way to Zion?" the man at the head of the crowd asked. It looked as if he had been crying. In fact the whole group had been weeping as they had been searching for the way to Zion for many years. Some had been devoured on the way; six million of them had perished as they passed through Germany to get to these mountains. They had faced many adversaries on their long journey and everyone they met on the way who realized they were seeking Zion had opposed them, often violently, yet a remnant survived, in fact two remnants survived, one group called Davidsons and another group called Ben-Israel.

"You are lost!" said an unhelpful voice from the train. "There is no way to Zion for you on this train; your shepherds have led you astray." Understandably considering the experiences of the past centuries (and these terrible words just uttered), they were suspicious of the train but they were desperate to find the way to Zion, so in the end they overcome their fears and asked the way.

"I am the way," said the driver of the train to everyone's astonishment. "Join this train and I will take you to Zion. Here is a ticket that is valid for a thousand years."

So the driver got out and gave everyone there who asked, a red ticket like the one Ian had. Each one kneeled down on the platform to receive their ticket. More tears flowed, tears of joy, all their tears from their long tortuous journey were wiped away, only tears of joy were left now.

They had escaped from the lady in scarlet who thought she was the queen of the mountains; they were safe now, finally.

A special carriage had been reserved for them. There were exactly the right number of seats for the new passengers, not one was missing, and no one had to stand. They at last had found the way to Zion.

The train had made quite a long detour to reach the scarlet mountains where these passengers had lost their way, but the driver was very happy to make this extra trip to find these precious passengers who had got lost and had suffered persecution for so much of their journey.

However, some of the passengers on board did not welcome them, thinking their special carriage had been scrapped years ago, and replaced by more modern carriages which were a different color, and rebranded by the Controller's son. But in fact the new carriages had been coupled to the old ones that were at the front, near the drivers cab. They had been empty (or almost empty) for a long time but were now full of joyous passengers singing the songs of Zion.

The driver had to speak to these passengers who had been less than welcoming. But after he had explained what had happened to them, and how he had saved them too, these passengers accepted the new arrivals and the train continued its journey to Zion as one.

The train to Zion continued its journey through the mountains into Switzerland and eventually pulled into Grindelwald.

There were busloads of tourists, mostly from China and South Korea, wanting to go to the "top of Europe". There had been a revival in both these countries so that the number of passengers on their way to Zion per head of population in both China and South Korea exceeded the number in Europe. There were also some from the USA, some from Japan, and a few from France. There were also a few from Saudi Arabia and Israel. When they saw the destination on the front of the train, "Zion," the Jews, and most of the Christians, were happy to get on, but people from other religions preferred to wait for another train, but all trains in this land are bound for Zion.

There was a queue to get on the train, even a little pushing and shoving to get the best views of the mountains, as the train was due to ascend up to the North face of the Eiger. Great views of the Eiger, Monch, Jungfrau, and Schreckhorn had been promised by the posters advertising the trip. In small text right at the foot of the notice it was written "for the best views please take the rear carriage." Well hardly anybody bothered to read this and nearly everyone rushed to get into the first carriage. It was quite a squash with over half the people standing, some trying to get close to the windows with their tele-photo lenses, others with giant rucksacks and ice axes; and others with children asleep in their backpacks oblivious to all the hubbub. An old couple from Austria had the last carriage to themselves.

Once the passengers had finally packed themselves onto the train in this most inhomogeneous manner, off it went (down not up). Five minutes later the train pulled into Grund, a station in the valley below Grindelwald. The engineers, who had built this section of track over a hundred years ago, had cleverly made the most of the steep terrain. They had laid the track in a Y shape to match the terrain, so that the trains pulled in from one side of the Y and went out on the other side of the Y. This meant of course that the order of the carriages got reversed, so the first were last and the last were first. The couple from Austria, who had read the poster at Grindelwald station carefully, had marvelous views right up to the top and plenty of space to enjoy it. Those crammed into the first carriage (now the last) saw very little, not only because it was the last carriage, but also because they were so squashed together they could hardly see past each other's armpits.

Ian now realized how true it was that the first shall be last and the last first. Many who Ian expected to be the first to catch the train to Zion were still in Talybont, or worse still, on the wrong train. Others who Ian expected to be the last to be seen dead on the train to Zion were in fact the first on board having been prepared to put to death their own selfishness, and had entered a new life on the continent after passing through the Channel Tunnel.

Chapter 32

The Final Stop

"How long will it take us to get to Zion?" Ian asked John Patmos, who, Ian realized, had just sat down next to them where Matthieu and Charles used to sit.

"It is revealed that it will be a thousand years, Ian," John replied.

"So I will have plenty of time to understand why everything happened as it did when I was in the UK then." Ian replied.

"Yes, and you will see how every trial had its purpose, every tear was needed, and how you were trained to be what you are now—a prince in the company of Zion. You have been granted authority by the Controller to rule for a thousand years in this land that he has conquered."

"What is the name of this land?" Ian asked.

"This land is called 'The New Kingdom of Eden', because it is like the original garden in Eden, but renewed. I am sure you remember the original one was spoilt by Adam, his wife and that serpent, the same one you saw bound in the tunnel before you crossed France and Germany."

"Will we see the tree of life?" Ian asked.

"Yes you will, and you will eat of that tree which will sustain you for a thousand years and more."

"What about the tree of the knowledge of good and evil?"

"Yes," replied John, "you will know and understand everything that the Controller did after the garden was spoilt, why the Rail Company was set up, why he had to send his own son, why not everybody wanted to be on the train, and why so many suffered in the other land.

"The tree of life shall bear much fruit, twelve different kinds of fruit and not only once a year but every month. Even the leaves of this tree are very precious; they are for the healing of the nations. There is a representative from every nation, every tribe, and every tongue, on the train to Zion and these leaves are the balm they need to be healed, ready for their arrival in Zion."

"WOW!" Ian exclaimed.

"Wonder of wonders indeed!" John replied.

The journey through France, Germany, Liechtenstein, and Switzerland took five hundred years. They visited every village, every mountain, and every chateau. They saw eagles, wild boar, and bears. They saw brilliant butterflies in Liechtenstein, lavender fields in Provence, snowflakes in Chamonix, as well as sunsets over the Mediterranean at Menton.

The next five hundred years took them through the rest of Europe and through Germany again. They saw all the romantic canals of Venice, beautiful church buildings, and tasted every delicacy ever prepared in that fair city. They heard all the works of Strauss in Vienna, all the works of Bach in Eisenach, and they even listened to lectures about general relativity in Ulm in Germany. There was nothing that anybody wanted to see or hear throughout Europe that they did not see or hear.

Ian could sing to his heart's content. These were his favorite songs during his first decade:-

- How Great Thou Art
- Amazing Grace
- Dear Lord and Father of Mankind
- When I survey the wondrous cross
- Be Thou my vision
- Thine be the glory
- Praise My Soul the King of Heaven
- Trust and Obey (When we walk with the Lord)
- Bread of Heaven (Guide me O thou great Redeemer)
- To be a pilgrim.

Next the train wound its way up a green hill with a distant view of a dark valley. This was where the last word of Yesha Yahu came to pass. Ian had not expected it, neither had his fellow passengers. At the previous stop some new passengers (mainly from one family—the Davidsons) had got on. They had been sent to declare glory amongst the nations and to bring as many of their brothers to the great house in the city of Zion as possible. The vessels that were to bring them home needed to be perfectly clean, so none of the old trains back in England, or even Wales, were good enough; only the trains cleaned by the Controller's son were good enough; he had sweated blood and tears to provide a clean train for these brothers. Now that this final group of passengers was on board, the next stop could be Zion itself. The train was full at last!

However, this was not the last word. As had been predicted hundreds of years ago the passengers now saw laid out before them miles and miles of corpses in the valley of Gehenna. These were those who had rebelled against the Controller, despite all that he had done for them. This is a place where the worms live forever and the fire never goes out. Ian found the sight abhorrent, shocking, not what he was expecting to see on the way to Zion, but there it was as clear as day for all to see. Ian checked in his book and yes, this was indeed what the Controller had said would happen to those who rebelled against Him.

The train then stopped at the last scheduled stop before its final destination. There was a magnificent view from the station. Two vast mountains could be seen in the distance; one looked golden, hardly distinguishable from the golden sand below, and the other blue, hardly distinguishable from the blue sky above. The Blue Mountain looked amazing, it looked unreal it was so beautiful; you could hardly imagine it was a physical mountain it looked so ethereal, so heavenly.

Looking up the line there was a distinct fork ahead, a track (in fact several tracks) to the left that led to the Golden Mountain, and a single track that led straight on to the Blue Mountain. Both sets of tracks went through the hot, dry desert, and then down into Death Valley, which was the hottest, lowest, driest place on earth. This was in fact the second Death Valley the train to Zion had visited. Ian could just about make out a tunnel entrance on the narrow track and a wide bridge over the valley towards the Golden Mountain. This was the second tunnel the train to Zion had to go through. Beyond Death Valley, both tracks were fenced off with high impenetrable fences, to stop lions and elephants getting onto the lines, and also to prevent anybody wandering onto the tracks. Ian thought only mad dogs and Englishmen would venture out in the heat of this desert, but maybe a foolhardy soul might try at night to follow the track under his own steam, to get to one of the mountains without getting on the train. Such a journey by foot looked impossible to Ian.

On the right, next to the narrow straight track, there was a collection of four buildings. Firstly, there was a great white building that looked like a hospital. There the blind, the deaf, the lame, the anxious, and the dumb were going in. Before long they appeared at the exit, the blind seeing, the deaf hearing, the lame dancing, the anxious laughing, and the dumb singing.

Next there was what looked like a music shop. In the window was a golden harp, but that was by no means the only instrument available. A photo of this shop window had appeared in an article about this last station in the Sunday supplement of the *Daily Times* newspaper, which is why Ian had supposed everyone would be given a harp before entering this final section of the journey. But this was a great underestimate of the generosity of the shopkeeper of this the last music shop in the land. Inside you could get trumpets, lyres, cymbals, flutes, and every kind of electric guitar. At the back of the shop was a kind of university music department. They taught everything there was to know about music for the soul. Thousands of songs had been written, and they were all available in vast books (or if you preferred you could get them on a music kindle that played all the tunes and showed all the words of every good song ever written).

The third building looked like a pottery shop. It was filled with large pots, like those that African women put on their heads to carry water. There were two kinds of pots available; one for water and one for oil. Everyone was encouraged to take with them enough oil for their lamps and water to drink for the final stage of the journey to Zion.

Finally, there was a building that looked like a ticket office, red brick-built, and very charming, like those old-fashioned stations in the country all covered with pretty flowers and gaily painted wood and metalwork. This was the place of redemption. This was where you redeemed your ticket. In exchange for showing your ticket, you were permitted to travel on the last leg of the journey to Zion—no turning back. Inside the building it looked more like a slaughterhouse, there was blood everywhere, yet those who went through this building onto the train were as clean as a whistle, as white as the neck of a swan, and as pure as the driven snow.

Only the perfect were allowed back on the train, but all those queuing up looked far from perfect to Ian. He knew many of them had done terrible things, robbed the rich, raged with anger, even murdered the innocent, and taken the wives of absent soldiers. Despite all this they had been made perfect. Their wrongs had been separated from them, the price for their imperfections had been paid; they were ransomed, redeemed, and free to travel on to Zion.

Then, a train drew up alongside the train to Zion. It was smart, beautifully clean on the outside, and shone like a golden mirror at midday. This train was full of people, all very smartly dressed and beautifully tanned, as if they were on the cover of *Vogue Magazine*.

Then to Ian's horror he saw the door of the train to Zion open and half a dozen passengers got out, exchanged their red ticket for a golden ticket and boarded the golden train. They too looked perfectly dressed for a night out at the opera, but Ian wondered how they would survive the journey through the desert ahead, dressed as they were.

There was a final announcement proclaiming the departure of the train to the Golden Mountain. To Ian the voice sounded recorded, obviously not live, it was machine-like, cold, without soul, so Ian was not tempted to change trains, even though the information was clear, precise, and perfectly pronounced.

Ian was then startled by what he thought was thunder. A rumbling from the Golden Mountain could indeed be heard, quite faint as it was so far away. Ian got out his binoculars to take a closer look at the Golden Mountain. What he saw was a fearful, awesome sight. There was a thick cloud on the top, fires burning lower down but Ian could not focus on the form of the mountain itself, not because of the optics of his binoculars but because the whole mountain was shaking. At the foot of the mountain Ian saw a massive golden fence to keep out anyone who might have reached that far on their own, but Ian could not make out anybody there. Ian saw the train line on the side of the mountain and a notice where the line crossed the fence saying: "Perfection only beyond this point." Who could ascend this holy hill, Ian thought to himself.

Then Ian's binoculars caught a glimpse of a fine golden thread emanating from the top of the Golden Mountain. Ian followed its line and it gently looped down towards a vast, deep chasm set between the Golden Mountain and the Blue Mountain. Directly above this chasm (in fact hundreds of meters above) it started to rise up again. Up, up it went and finally Ian saw that it was attached to the top of the Blue Mountain. On closer examination, Ian realized it was a kind of rope-bridge between the two mountain peaks, made of golden thread, and very narrow indeed. Not a bridge for anyone overweight or suffering from vertigo!

Ian then saw the bridge gently wobbling up and down and side to side. Ian attached a special pair of lenses to his binoculars to focus in on what was causing this. Someone was walking across the rope-bridge. No, in fact it looked like three people. First was one who looked like the Controller's son, then Moshe and Elias. Behind them Ian thought he could make out a few more figures, but he wasn't sure. Could these be the famous Enoch who walked with the Controller for 365 years in the first complete walk along the entire rail track centuries earlier, and the great king of Salem who famously received the first ever gift to the Rail Charity (Ab had given him 10 percent of his bonus when he completed the first ever rail line in the nine kingdoms from Shinar to Zeboiim). Ian watched anxiously as they slowly walked this tightrope. He was so relieved when they all made it safely to the Blue Mountain.

As the golden train departed Ian noticed that it was not in fact as perfect as it first appeared, he could see some rust marks, some black smoke, and mold on the edges of the door to the catering carriage.

Ian watched as it went down into the second Death Valley. Here it entered the last leg of its journey. Its passengers expected this golden train to bring them to the Golden Mountain, but it could not. There was a great fire in this valley and all flesh was burnt up. Nothing man-made survived, cotton clothes burnt, polyester and nylon clothes quickly melted; even iron and steel perished in the flames.

All those who had bought the golden ticket to travel on this train were burnt. It had been very hard to earn enough to buy a ticket for this train; the application form had ten commandments that each applicant had to sign to say they had obeyed them all, plus an annex about loving your neighbor as yourself and loving the Controller. Notes had been added by some lawyers over the years to help applicants to fill in the form correctly, these notes ran to 100 pages and few read them all. Nevertheless some had signed the form, handed over their money, and hoped to be transported over the second Death Valley by means of this golden train. Even some from the train to Zion had been tempted by the golden train.

Then Ian turned his binoculars to the Blue Mountain. The narrow rail track leading towards the Blue Mountain had a high fence on each side, just like the fence on the other track to the Golden Mountain. It was there to keep lions, jackals, and serpents from attacking the passengers in the train to Zion, and to stop the foolhardy (those who had sold their souls to gain all the riches of the earth but did not have a ticket to ride on the train to Zion) from attempting to jump on the moving train on the last leg of its journey, without a ticket.

This line also went through the desert, but before it went down into the second Death Valley Ian could see lots of different colors next to the line. Peering down the lenses Ian eventually worked out they were flowers growing on the line-side, purple crocuses, the rose of Sharon, and lily of the valley. These were growing next to a little stream fed from springs of fresh water welling up from deep within the Blue Mountain itself.

Then, like the other line to the Golden Mountain, it dropped into the second Death Valley. It was so steep it cast a shadow over the plain, and there, in the shadow of the valley of death, Ian saw what he thought was the Controller himself, along with a scepter and a shepherd's staff. He also saw a table laid out with every good thing to sustain the traveler. The table was in full view of the jackals, the lions, and the snakes, but Ian could see the Controller protecting the table from these thieving animals. There was oil there too and balm. A cup overflowed with the most refreshing fruit juice you could imagine, made from the seven fruits grown by the Controller. It looked like this was the final place of refreshment before entering the tunnel.

But before Ian had time to work out where the tunnel led, or how long it was, or how wide it was, he was jolted by the train to Zion setting off on its final part of the journey. It went through the desert, past the flowers, down into the valley where it briefly stopped at the Controller's table where all the passengers took their final food and drink before entering the final tunnel. This was the second tunnel the train to Zion had passed through. It was much longer and darker than the first tunnel (the Channel Tunnel).

At the entrance to the tunnel the train had to go through what looked like a great fire, similar on first impressions to the one on the line to the Golden Mountain. However, once inside it was different, instead of intense heat there was intense sound and vibration, like on the test track back in Kent, but much more intense. Every conceivable type of shaking was taking place. There was rocking like a ship being tossed about in a great storm, there was a deep booming like the sound of an alpine horn, there was a sharp screeching sound, a squealing as the train rounded a bend, a vibration like a road being repaired, a high-pitched siren, ultrasonic vibrations like those used to clean teeth, and finally microwaves which vibrated every water molecule—even the very cells that make up the human body. Everything was shaken that could be shaken, so that nothing remained other than that which could not be shaken. All flesh was destroyed by this shaking. All that survived was pure soul.

Then suddenly the shaking was over and a bright light came on inside the train in the tunnel. Every soul on the train was now shining white like the sun. The train itself had survived this shaking but was now totally red, crimson blood red, no other color could be seen anywhere on the train.

Then the train emerged on the other side of the tunnel, up the far side of the second Death Valley, with not a single passenger lost.

Now was the time to celebrate! Out came the instruments; out came the song sheets, singing, dancing, laughter, joy, and gladness. Through the windows of the train, all the passengers could now see the Blue Mountain getting bigger and bigger. Jars of water, some of which had turned into wine, were emptied into overflowing cups. Oil from other jars was poured into the quaint old lamps that kept a strangely bright light burning inside the carriages at night. The oil was also used to fuel the engine of the train. No more coal, no more soot, and no more smoke here.

Then each passenger was given a piece of wood. "What are these for?" everyone was asking. Then an announcement came over the tannoy explaining that they were scepters. Each one was crafted from wood from Calvary (a hill just outside Jerusalem), acacia wood, and each person had his name written on their own piece. Some also had jewels set within the wood, others were silver-coated or gold-coated, and others still were stained with blood and tears.

Then a voice spoke to everyone on the train to Zion: "Before you sit down to rest for ever in the heavenly city of Zion, you have one last task. You will show how to live. You have learnt how to live now, you have overcome, you have been tried and tested, and have come through refined and perfected. You are to build a perfect rail line this side of the Valley of Death on the foothills of the Blue Mountain. There will be no more tears, no more crying, no more sighing, no more regulations, no more grumpy passengers, no more false announcements, no more illness, no more death, only this wonderful task that you were made for; to rebuild the rail line in New Kingdom of Eden."

With everyone working together in perfect harmony following the Controller's instructions in spirit as well as to the letter, they soon completed the perfect rail line, just south of the Blue Mountain after the valley of Gehenna.

Eventually they left the awesome sight of the valley of Gehenna and the wonderful Blue Mountain, and arrived at the border of Zion, where they could see, towering above, the city of Zion itself! A city set on a hill, a separate hill. Zion is the home of the Controller, where he lives.

Also on Mount Zion they saw the Lamb with 144,000 next to Him. The other train Ian had seen in Calais must have arrived in Zion ahead of them. Every one of them had their names written in the book of life, and the name of the Lamb was written on their foreheads. This crowd was cheering at the sight of the train approaching. Then they started to gather together all the citizens of Zion to prepare a proper welcome for Ian and his fellow passengers.

On Mount Zion a stone, a cornerstone, a precious stone could now be seen. Some had thought this was a stumbling block, a great barrier to entering the great city, but in fact it was the way in. There was a golden rope attached to this stone. It was said that you had to put your whole trust in the rope and in the stone, believing that it was not going to topple over under your weight; this was the way to enter the city of Zion.

The train was arriving at Zion, the heavenly Jerusalem. There was a massive crowd there now cheering joyously as the train pulled ever closer. Some in the crowd were all dressed in white, like the messengers Ian had seen occasionally, earlier in his journey. Others in the crowd were fellow passengers who had arrived before Ian, and were already perfected and accepted as citizens of Zion. At the head of the crowd were the Controller and his son, whose blood had been shed to pay for the tickets to Zion. In fact he had paid for many more tickets than were ever used. Only a few had realized how important their offer of a free ticket to Zion was. Most had ignored it or despised the offer. But the son had paid the full price for every single person ever born on the earth to have a ticket to Zion.

The son wore robes dyed red with his own blood, and he wore a crown of thorns. The crown no longer hurt but reminded everybody of the price he had paid to secure safe passage to Zion for those on Ian's train.

The son had been appointed King of Zion, but despite this he still continued to ride about the city on a little donkey, the same one he rode on his way to his death on the other side.

All Israel were there too. The savior of the sons of Israel came from Zion and had returned to Zion. He had achieved his mission of removing godlessness from Israel. His own brothers were there, some half-brothers had deserted him but all his true brothers were there.

And so with great songs of rejoicing from all those assembled on the walls of Mount Zion the train approached within a mile of the city of Zion.

Chapter 33

The Last Mile

IAN WAS LOOKING OUT of the window and looking forward to finally arriving at his destination. He wondered what the last mile would be like. He was still concerned for Matthieu and Charles as he hadn't seen them for ages. Just then Angi came and sat next to him, and offered to explain to him what happens during the last mile. She was dressed all in white, had bright blonde hair and a shining complexion. She was not young; she had seen many things before on the journey to Zion. She seemed to see things from a different perspective, the long-term strategy, the big picture. I guess that is why she was head of communications for the Rail Company.

Angi explained, ". . . after a thousand years the train finally leaves the last station on its approach to the ultimate destination: Zion."

"What will it be like?" Ian asked, "how will we get in?"

"In three and a half years all will be revealed," said Angi.

Here is what Angi revealed to Ian as they traveled the last mile of the journey to Zion:-

"The city of Zion is twelve hundred miles wide, twelve hundred miles long and twelve hundred miles high," said Angi.

"And the walls are 144 feet thick. There are twelve gates into the city, each one named after one of the twelve rail divisions. The gates are made of enormous pearls.

"A pearl is created through the suffering of an oyster—a piece of grit inside its shell causes the beautiful mother of pearl to be formed around it, transforming the grit into an object of great beauty. In the same way the ancient passengers on the train to Zion have suffered over the centuries yet they have overcome by the grace of God. So the gates of the holy city, Zion, are made from twelve giant pearls; one for each rail division. Twelve thousand from this ancient people have already entered the city through these gates. But one division is missing. Nobody from Dan is there; there is no gate with Dan's name on it. He failed to overcome. Dan, which means 'judged', has been replaced by Manasseh, which means 'God has made me forget all my trouble'. Grace has triumphed over judgment. This shows that you can't take your place in the city of God for granted, even if you are one of the very sons of Jake as Dan was.

"It was the same with the friends who the Controller's son chose to follow him, who became company board members. One of them was lost, Jude, and he had to be replaced, by Matt. This team of messengers had to be twelve again before the Controller could start the final phase of his work on the rail system."

"There do seem to be a lot of twelves in the city of Zion," remarked Ian.

"Yes," said Angi, "twelve divisions of the ancient rail system have their names on the pearly gates and the twelve friends who were sent out by the Controller's son, at great cost, to bring good news to the whole world are the foundations of the walls of the city. And you will also see the twelve fruits on the tree of life, fruiting twelve times each year. Twelve times twelve thousand from the twelve divisions that went ahead. Even the dimensions of the city itself are multiples of twelve. This shows how precious the sufferings of his ancient people are to the Controller and also how the sufferings of the people of the new covenant underpin Zion. Without these pearly gates nobody could enter the city. Without the foundations there would have been nothing to build on."

"What exactly was the new covenant built on? What was the foundation?" Ian asked Angi, wanting to clear up something that had puzzled him ever since he had left the UK for the continent of Europe. Ian had heard many people say the foundation was Oriog Jones, but it had always seemed odd to Ian that the new covenant should be built on just one frail human being.

"You were right to wonder." said Angi. "That misunderstanding came from something the Controller's son said in Caesarea Philippi to Oriog Jones.[32] He was reported to have said upon this 'petra,' literally 'large rock, bedrock or foundation stone,' I will build my new building. Many thought he meant Oriog himself, because Oriog also means rock, but Oriog literally is 'petros' a *small* stone or pebble, not a *foundation* stone at all. Oriog was blessed because the Controller had revealed to him who the Controller's son was and Petros, or Oriog as he was known in Wales, was the first person ever to say this out loud. It was this revelation spoken out that was actually the bedrock, the foundation, on which the new building, the new covenant, was to be built. In other words not a person at all, but the principle of listening to God, only speaking and acting on what God reveals, not doing your own thing, and not looking to one human individual who one moment is commended, and the next seeks to spread fear, and so has to be rebuked by the Controller's son in the strongest terms with the words: 'Get behind me Satan!'

"This was Jake's family problem too, they wanted their own driver rather than the Controller as their leader; they worshipped other controllers in addition to the true Controller. They dwelt in paneled houses when the station lay neglected and dilapidated. Even Ab made this mistake. He wanted to create the child the Controller had promised him, so he committed adultery, took a slave girl, and this 'child of the flesh' lead to all sorts of problems over the centuries. If only he had built his house on the foundation exactly as the Controller had said—by faith.

"Look you can see these gates and foundations of the city of Zion right now! Do you understand their meaning now?!" exclaimed Angi to Ian.

Ian paused still not sure, so Angi asked: "What do you see built on the foundations?"

"Jewels," replied Ian. "Twelve different jewels, each with a different color including amethyst, jasper, and emerald."

"These are the suffering people of the Rail Company who have overcome," said Angi.

"Do you know how jewels get their color, Ian?" asked Angi.

"No, tell me," said Ian.

"Pure undistorted crystal structures have a band gap that is greater that the energy of visible light, but these jewels had stress applied because of extra atoms in their structure and they strain to accommodate these visitors. These 'defects' in the crystal structure are what leads to lower energy band gaps, so that when pure white light shines through these jewels the electrons inside the atoms move around absorbing some of the energy that give the jewels their distinctive color. Each type of defect leads to one type of beauty, one color. So just as the grit in the pearl led to beauty in the material of the gates of Zion, so the stress and strain of the crystals adorning the foundations led to the beautiful variety of colors you now see shining from these gems. The trials that the people of the new building endured over the centuries are like this stress and strain. Of course you can only see the jewels' beauty when the pure white light shines on them."

Ian wondered if there would be a terminal station within the city of Zion. He assumed it would be a temple or a church. But no, Angi explained that there is no temple and no church building in the holy city of Zion. No physical building.

"You can't go to church, you can't go to the true Temple," said Angi.

"The physical temple was just a shadow of this, a picture. The church is the body of the Controller's son, his people, not a building!" exclaimed Angi.

"So that is why there are no buildings in Zion, not even a station. But the train is there."

Then in marched Matthieu and Charles beaming with joy. They had had the time of their lives. Ian was so pleased to see them again and share in their joy.

Despite being on the train to Zion for just over a thousand years Ian was not weary of it. But now, before he had time to catch up with Matthieu and Charles, the train came to a halt within the city of Zion and the Controller announced that the way into the city was clear. The time had arrived to alight from the train.

So Ian collected up his few remaining belongings, his ticket, his white stone, the book of the Rail Company, and his wedding outfit. And together with his cousin Dafydd, his friends Nick, Gareth, Methedig, Matthieu, and Charles, he walked through the carriage to the train door for the last time. Ian was about to say goodbye to his fellow passengers when he realized that they were, of course, all coming too and that he would have forever to talk to them about their journeys, his journey, and the journeys of everyone who had arrived safely in Zion. So Ian just thanked them for their company, and that, surely, was all he needed to do.

There was no time to be lost before Ian set off to explore the city of Zion, or so he thought. In fact there was no *time* there at all; he had all the time in the world, what bliss; no rush, no deadlines, no collapse into chaos and disorder, no more work. He could now rest, enjoy life in all its fullness, forever.

The city was brilliant, as brilliant as crystal clear jasper. As Angi had explained during the last mile, it did indeed have a great high wall (144 feet high), with twelve gates where there were twelve messengers dressed in white. The twelve gates were made out of twelve separate giant pearls and on them were written the names of the sons (and one grandson) of

Jake: Judah, Reuben, Gad, Asher, Naphtali, Manasseh, Simeon, Levi, Issachar, Zebulun, Joe, and Benjamin. The wall was supported by twelve foundation stones, the twelve friends of the Controller's son who were sent to proclaim good news: Oriog, Andrew Jones, James (the son of Zebedee), John Four, Philip, Bartholomew Nathanael, Thomas, Matthieu, Levi, James (the son of Alphaeus), Thaddaeus, Simon the Zealot, and Matt (who had replaced Jude). Each stone was made of a different jewel: jasper, sapphire, agate, emerald, onyx, ruby, chrysolite, beryl, topaz, turquoise, jacinth, and amethyst.[33]

The city of Zion was 12,000 by 12,000 miles wide (144 million square miles) paved with pure gold.

Ian walked on the gold pavement, and despite Angi's words to him, started looking for the golden temple that he had read about, but it was nowhere to be found. Then Ian remembered that there was no need for a temple in Zion. Ian looked up; there was no sun, no moon, and no stars, yet it was brighter than the brightest day. There was no night there. The gates never closed—anyone who had accepted a ticket from the Controller's son could enter at any time.

Every nation's culture had been incorporated into Zion. The place was spotless; there was nothing unclean there at all. Only those whose names were written in the book of life were there, none of the followers of the lady of Babylon were there, nor were there any there who had tricked their way in (that was impossible).

At the top of the city, in the middle of the street, Ian saw a throne on which sat the Controller's son, who had the appearance of a lamb, and out of there a river flowed that was the lifeblood of all those who lived in the city. On either side of the river there were the twelve trees that Angi had told him about.

Everybody could see the Controller whenever they wanted. So with boldness Ian approached the throne where the Controller was seated and was offered a crown, which he gladly accepted. He said to Ian, "Well done, good and faithful traveler! You have been faithful with a few things; I will put you in charge of many things. Enter into the joy of your Controller!"

The inhabitants of this city, however, didn't call Him "Controller" they called Him Yahweh Jireh (the Lord my Provider), Yahweh Rapha (the Lord my Healer), Yahweh Nissi (the Lord my Banner), Yahweh Shalom (the Lord my Peace), Yahweh Ra'ah (the Lord my Shepherd), Yahweh Tsidkenu (the Lord my Righteousness), and Yahweh Shammah (the Lord is here).[34] And his Son they called Wonderful Counsellor, Mighty God, Everlasting Father, Prince of Peace, the Lamb, the Bridegroom, the Good Shepherd, the King of Kings, the Root of David, the Bright Morning Star, the Messiah, and the Word.

You have come to Mount Zion, even to the city of the living God, the heavenly Jerusalem.[35]

The End.

Endnotes

1. Newton, *Amazing Grace*
2. Sulman, *Engraving of vicarage*
3. Hughes, *Cwm Rhondda*
4. Engber, *How Dangerous Is Hail?*
5. Gammons, *The Seven Redemptive Names of God*, 13
6. Slick, *What is the Gospel?* lines 1–33
7. Isa 62:12
8. Carter, *Jehovah's Witnesses*, 3
9. Isa 59:2, 53:6 & 12b
10. Gen 11:4
11. Ps 40:6 (NKJV)
12. 1 Cor 15:3 (Author version)
13. Jas 2:26b
14. Jude 1:24–25
15. Newton, *Amazing Grace*
16. Marsh, *Train*, 14
17. Wordsworth, *I wandered lonely as a cloud*
18. Woods, *Level crossing accidents*
19. John 14:6
20. Matt 10:28b
21. Luke 6:38
22. 2 Cor 9:6
23. Deut 32:35
24. Matt 5:39
25. John 3:16
26. Mark 10:52
27. Betjeman, *Slough*
28. Welch, *Thomas Theme Lyrics*
29. Luke 6:38
30. Matt 19:19b
31. Rev 17:5
32. Matt 16:18–23
33. Rev 21:1–20
34. Gammons, *The Seven Redemptive Names of God,* 2
35. Heb 12:22a

Bibliography

Betjeman, John. "Slough." In *Continual Dew*, London, John Murray, 1937. https://en.wikipedia.org/wiki/Slough_(poem).

Carter, Joe. *Nine Things You Should Know About Jehovah's Witnesses,* item 3, The Gospel Coalition, 29th April 2016. https://www.thegospelcoalition.org/article/9-things-you-should-know-about-jehovahs-witnesses/.

Engber, Daniel. "How Dangerous Is Hail?" In *Slate News and Politics*, April 3rd 2006. https://slate.com/news-and-politics/2006/04/how-dangerous-is-hail.html.

Gammons, Peter. *The Seven Redemptive Names of God*, Orlando, Peter Gammons Ministries International, 2017. https://pgmi.org.

Hughes, John. *Cwm Rhondda*, 1905. https://en.wikipedia.org/wiki/Cwm_Rhondda.

Marsh, Philip. *Train: The Evolution of Rail Travel,* 14, London, Carlton Books, 2015.

Newton, John. *Amazing Grace*, 1779, from https://library.timelesstruths.org/music/Amazing_Grace/ and http://www.godvine.com/Elvis-Presley-Sings-a-Wonderful-Version-of-Amazing-Grace-70.html.

Slick, Matt. *What is the Gospel?* 23rd November 2008. https://carm.org/what-gospel.

Sulman, T. *Engraving of the vicarage at Olney where John Newton spent his first years as a minister,* 1879. https://commons.wikimedia.org/wiki/File:Olney_vicarage.jpg.

Welch, Ed. *Thomas Theme Lyrics.* Lyrics.com. STANDS4 LLC, 2020. Web. September 15th 2020. https://www.lyrics.com/lyric/5791400.

Woods, Michael. *Research into the causes of pedestrian accidents at level crossings and potential solutions- RSSB Research Brief,* 1, 2014. https://catalogues.rssb.co.uk/library/research-development-and-innovation/research-brief-T984.pdf.

Wordsworth, William. "I Wandered Lonely as a Cloud." In *Poems in Two Volumes*, Longman, Hurst, Rees, Orme, 1807.

www.ingramcontent.com/pod-product-compliance
Lightning Source LLC
Chambersburg PA
CBHW050403030726
47503CB00006B/1990